ULTIMATE ENDING

BOOK 2

THE HOUSE
ON
HOLLOW HILL

Check out the full

ULTIMATE ENDING BOOKS

Series:

TREASURES OF THE FORGOTTEN CITY

THE HOUSE ON HOLLOW HILL

THE SHIP AT THE EDGE OF TIME

ENIGMA AT THE GREENSBORO ZOO

THE SECRET OF THE AURORA HOTEL

THE STRANGE PHYSICS OF THE HEIDELBERG LABORATORY

THE TOWER OF NEVER THERE

Cover design by Milan Jaram www.MilanJaram.com

Internal artwork by Jaime Buckley www.jaimebuckley.com

Enjoyed this book? Please take the time to leave a review on Amazon.

To Connor Schulte,
who will someday choose his own adventure.

Welcome to **Ultimate Ending,**
where YOU choose the story!

That's right – everything that happens in this book is a result of
decisions YOU make. So choose wisely!

But also be careful. Throughout this book you'll find tricks and traps,
trials and tribulations! Most you can avoid with common sense and a
logical approach to problem solving. Others will require a little bit of luck.
Having a coin handy, or a pair of dice, will make your adventure even more
fun. So grab em' if you got em'!

Along the way you'll also find tips, clues, and even items that can help
you in your quest. You'll meet people. Pick stuff up. Taking note of these
things is often important, so while you're gathering your courage, you
might also want to grab yourself a pencil and a sheet of paper.

Keep in mind, there are *many* ways to end the story. Some conclusions
are good... some not so good.
Some of them are even great!
But remember:

There is only *ONE*

ULTIMATE ENDING!

THE HOUSE ON HOLLOW HILL

Welcome to the House on Hollow Hill!

You are MIKE THOMPSON, a highschooler in upstate New York. You're walking down the street with your friends Emma and Jake, admiring the autumn leaves on the trees lining the neighborhood.

Jake lets out a big sigh. "Let's go back to the field," he says, tossing a baseball back and forth with himself. "I want to practice my curveball."

Emma laughs. "You're the only kid who spends all day at school and wants to go back for more."

"I don't want to go back to *school,* I want to go back to the field *outside* of the school." He turns to you. "Come on Mike, you promised you'd play catch."

You shake your head at him. "I'll play catch with you this weekend. I need to get home and practice the piano." You have a test for music class tomorrow.

Jake sighs dramatically. "That's not what you promised."

"Leave off, Jake," Emma says. "I'm in Mrs. Baramule's class and have to practice too. She's strict! Can you believe she failed my sister for confusing a C with a C-sharp?" She rolled her eyes to let you know what she thought about *that.*

"Fine. But the next time you need help with anything..."

8

The massive house on the corner, old and decrepit, looms over you. "I heard old Mr. Goosen is moving out," you say.

Emma says, "Wow. He's lived in that house his whole life."

"He looks like he's lived there an entire *century,*" Jake says.

Suddenly there is a voice behind you. "Most of a century, in fact!" says Mr. Goosen. You whirl to face him and he smiles. He's wearing a tweed jacket on top of overalls, and his white hair hangs down his back. "Eighty-one years, to be exact."

Jake looks embarrassed, but you grin. Mr. Goosen has always been nice to you. "Is it true?" you ask. "You and your wife are going to move out?"

"We already have," he says, staring up at the massive three-story house. He shoves his hands in his pockets and looks strangely sad. "All that's left are things I can't take with me."

"Can't take with you?" Jake asks. "You mean you've left stuff inside the house? For anyone?"

"Yes, there's still plenty left in the house. I have too much stuff, you know, from all my adventures. I don't know what will happen to it all, now." Mr. Goosen is a well-known traveler: African safaris, scaling the Himalayas. He's done it all!

"You must be sad to leave so much," Emma says.

"Not at all," he replies. "The most important things are the memories! Got them all up here." He taps the side of his head.

Jake frowns with concentration. "Well if you're not taking them, and you don't know what's going to happen to them..."

"Jake!" Emma yells.

Mr. Goosen breaks out in a big smile. "Actually, that's exactly what I wanted to talk to you about..."

"I have one daughter and four grandkids, and they've already taken what they wanted. Everything else is going to be destroyed!"

"Destroyed?" Emma asks.

"The person who bought my house wants to build a new one," he says. "They're going to bulldoze the old one and everything inside." Mr. Goosen looks stricken by the thought.

"That's terrible!" you say.

Mr. Goosen points at you. "Yes, it is. I'd hate for everything to go to waste... so how would you like to keep something from inside? As a thank you for always being such good neighborhood kids?"

"Yeah!" Jake blurts out. He suddenly looks suspicious, and begins rolling his baseball between his fingers. "What's the catch?"

"No catch at all, son," Mr. Goosen says. "You three can go inside and take something before the bulldozers come."

"When are the bulldozers coming?" you ask.

Mr. Goosen pulls out a gold pocket watch, with a long chain connecting to his belt. It looks extremely valuable, with fine engraving on the back. "First thing tomorrow morning. So you have plenty of time."

Plenty of time? You and Emma have to practice for your music test! You both look at one-another. "Maybe if we just take a quick look..." Emma says.

"Oh, so you won't throw the ball with me, but you'll explore Mr. Goosen's house!" Jake says.

"You mean you don't want to go inside?" you ask.

Jake's frown turns into a toothy grin. "Okay, you got me. Of course I do!"

"Well then it's settled!" Mr. Goosen exclaims, throwing his hands in the air. "The doors are locked, but the key is in the mailbox. OH! I almost forgot. I have many trinkets and treasures throughout my house, but you must promise me you will only take *one thing*. It can be any item of special value, but once you choose to take something, that's it!"

"Just one?" Jake says. "Aww."

You all turn to look at the house. It looks like something out of a scary movie, dark and ominous.

"Good luck!" Mr. Goosen calls. "And remember, just one item!" He sounds farther away. You turn to thank him one last time... and he's gone! The three of you spin around, looking down each street, but he's nowhere in sight.

"Wow, he must have been in a hurry to move," you say.

Jake runs to the mailbox and returns with an old, iron key, red with rust. In his other hand is a rolled-up piece of paper.

10

"Hey look, it's a map of the house!"

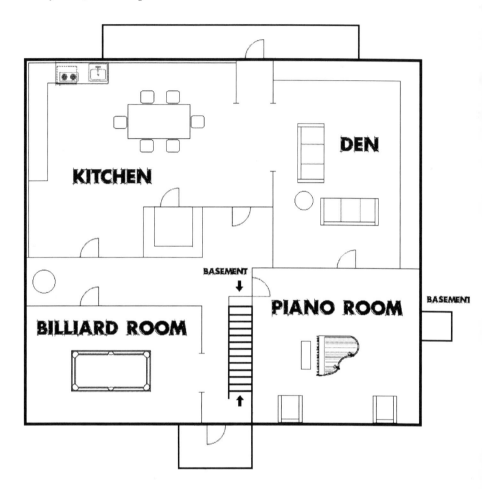

"Coooool," Jake says. "A billiard room? I bet there's some cool antique weapons in there. Like a battle ax or something. There's always cool stuff like that in a billiard room."

Emma looks concerned. "Where's the rest of the map?"

"Huh?" Jake asks.

"This is just the first floor," Emma says, tapping the page. "The house has two stories and a basement."

Jake gives an elaborate shrug. "Who cares? We can find our way around. It's not *that* big."

You take the key and look at the house. The front porch is dilapidated, with holes in the steps and spiderwebs in the corners. The door looks like it hasn't been opened in over a year. "Which way do you want to go inside?" you ask.

"What do you mean?" Jake says. "We've got the key, let's go in the front door."

"I don't know, it looks dangerous." You point to the side of the house, where there's a small path between the wall and the woods. "We could try around back. The map says there's a back door."

Emma says, "Or the basement. My mom and I used to help Mrs. Goosen move boxes around in the winter."

To keep things simple, open the front door *ON PAGE 19*

If you want to check the basement, *TURN TO PAGE 32*

If you'd rather try the backyard, *TURN TO PAGE 14*

12

The shadow approaches. You're about to bolt when you recognize his face. "Mr. Goosen!"

"You scared us!" Emma says.

He spreads his hands apologetically. "Didn't mean to! I tried to say hello first, but I think the thunder muffled my words."

You sigh with relief. "What are you doing out here?"

"Oh, just taking one last look at my property. The rain chased me in here. As for what chased *you* in here... that was the rare Atraharsi Weeping Vine. Most botanists believe it to be extinct, but I managed to recover some bulbs in my travels."

"It grew like a monster!" Jake says.

"Yes, yes. Well. It is quite rare, and quite *dangerous*, which is what makes it most exciting!" His smile disappears. "Unfortunately, what is not exciting is that you three have left my house without retrieving a prize from inside."

You realize he's right. "We can wait until the rain stops and go back inside." Jake and Emma share a skeptical look. It appears they've had enough for one night.

"I'm afraid that's against the rules," Mr. Goosen says. He pulls out his gold pocket watch and considers the time. "You had one chance, and that chance is over. Come on now. Let's get you three back home."

He leads you through the woods around the side of the house. The rain has let up by then, so that it's barely a drizzle. The sound of thunder booms in the distance as the storm rolls across the land.

"This is as far as I go," he says, standing just at the edge of the woods. "You three can make it home yourselves, I trust?"

You don't know why, but it feels like you're abandoning Mr. Goosen. "Are you sure we can't go back inside?"

"I'm sorry, Mike. Perhaps another time."

The three of you say goodbye and head home. You walk in silence, still processing everything you've seen: ghosts, killer vines, and so much more. If you had a chance to do it over again you *know* you would end up with a great prize! Unfortunately, though, you have reached...

THE END

The voice jolts you back to reality. "Yeah, I'm coming!" you call up to them.

You round the stairs and begin to climb. The boards creak noisily, a reminder that you just fell through a hole in the floor and landed on the piano. The wood better not break!

But that's the least of your worries. Three steps above you a white shape floats through the wood, stopping in the air. It's a little girl. Except she's transparent. She's...

"You're a ghost!" you blurt out.

She puts her hands on her hips. "You guys are bad at this, so I wanted to give you a clue!"

"A clue?" you ask, dumbfounded.

"A clue!" she agrees. "Listen closely, because I'm only going to tell you once. 'The path to what you THINK is most precious, is underneath what is TRULY most precious.' Got it?"

"I think so," you say. "Can you repeat it?"

"I said I'd only tell you once! You need to listen better!" And after the scolding she continues floating upwards, disappearing through the second floor ceiling.

Woah. Better find your friends *ON PAGE 67*

14

"I've got a funny feeling about the front door," you insist. "Let's check out the back yard."

Jake puts his glove up protectively. "Fine. Back yard it is."

They let you take the lead down the side of the house, brushing past untrimmed tree limbs. You walk past the cellar door and into the back yard. The lawn–which looks like it hasn't been mowed since before lawnmowers were invented–is brown and cracked. A long deck runs along the entire length of the house, with a single set of steps and a door leading inside.

Thankful that it's past tick season, you trudge through the tall grass and lead your friends up the three steps onto the deck. You can't see anything through the grimy windows, and the door has none, besides. You turn the brass knob on the door.

Locked!

You jiggle it two or three times before Emma coughs behind you. "Mike, the key..."

"Oh, right," you say, fishing it out of your pocket. You have to jam it into the lock to make it fit, it's so rusted. You just know it's never going to open the door, no matter how hard you–

The key turns and the lock clicks open. It worked!

You push the door open and it gives way about an inch before bumping into something. You push, leaning your weight, but it just won't budge.

"Maybe if you spent more time at the ball field you'd be able to open it," Jake chides. But he takes a turn on the door and has no greater success than you did. "I told you we should have gone through the front door."

Feeling stubborn, you say, "Out of the way." You take a few steps back, set your feet, and lower your shoulder.

Charge at the door and *TURN TO PAGE 17*

You throw back the shower curtain, grab Emma, and hop inside. Jake follows and closes the curtain behind you.

"Why'd we hide in here?" she hisses.

You put a finger to your lips. Jake nods his head vigorously.

You hear running water and a smacking wet sound, like a fish being thrown onto land. It happens two, three, four times in a row, along with an unmistakable suction sound. You can hear your heart beating against your temple. It's so loud you're sure whatever that thing is can hear it too!

The thing slides across the floor. For a moment you fear it might come toward the bathtub, but then you realize it's moving away. Then the sound changes, scraping on wood instead of tile. Slowly it grows distant until it stops altogether.

You wait another 30 seconds before nodding to your friends and stepping out from behind the curtain.

The floor is covered in water now, except the water is sticky, like glue. It's difficult to lift your shoe because of the substance. "I told you I heard something creepy!" you tell your friends.

Jake isn't making jokes now. "I don't think we should be here anymore," he says. "I want to go home."

"That's probably a good idea," you say, but a light appears at the edge of your vision. It's coming from inside the toilet!

Your friends take a step back, but you approach, strangely unafraid. You lean forward and peer into the toilet...

And see a glowing round object at the bottom. Mesmerized by the light, you're unable to stop yourself from reaching...

Reach inside the toilet by *FLIPPING TO PAGE 101*

16

"Let's wait here for Mrs. Hollencamp," you decide. "We'll just explain to her that Mr. Goosen allowed us to go into his house."

Emma nods as if it were the right thing to do. Jake looks scared. Realizing he's still holding the ax, he quickly tosses it back behind the door to the cellar.

You hear the sound of her Yorkie before you see them round the corner. "Ahh ha!" Mrs. Hollencamp says, pointing a wrinkled finger at you. "I knew I heard someone back here." She looks from one face to another. "Now this is quite a surprise. I would have expected this from Jake, but Mike? And *Emma*?"

Emma waits patiently for her to finish. She puts on her most polite voice. "This is a simple misunderstanding. We just spoke to Mr. Goosen, and he said we could go inside his house one last time before it was bulldozed."

The old woman looks taken aback. "When did Mr. Goosen give you permission?"

"Just now. Five minutes ago."

Mrs. Hollencamp's face twists in anger. "This is not funny. *Not funny at all.* I cannot believe you children you play such a cruel, distasteful joke. Especially so soon after Mr. Goosen..."

"No, it's true!" Emma sputters. "We're not making a joke at all!"

Mrs. Hollencamp reaches forward and grabs your arm. She has a surprising grip for a grandmother. "Come with me. We're going to go explain this to your parents and see what they say!"

Jake bolts for the back yard, but Emma sullenly follows Mrs. Hollencamp as she leads you down the street. Maybe Jake will have more fun inside the house, but for you two this is...

THE END

You close the short distance and hit the door square with your shoulder.

And you bounce right off.

Stumbling backwards, you slip and fall onto the wooden deck with a *thump*. Emma rushes to your side.

"Mike! Are you okay?"

You rub your shoulder. "Yeah, just fine." The worst thing harmed is your pride. You get to your feet and look around. "How else can we get inside? Should we go back to the front door?"

"You could try jumping through a window, stuntman," Jake says.

Ignoring him, you take a step back and look at the side of the house. You *might* be able to break a window if you found a rock or a brick, but the glass looks awfully thick. There's a balcony on the second story, and some windows to the left. And below the windows...

"Hey, check out that lattice."

There's a thick wooden lattice nailed against the house, spanning the entire wall from the ground to the second floor. It's covered in vines. "Those are actually pretty strong," Emma says. "My aunt has them on her house. They're bolted into the wall, to support all the weight of the plants."

The lattice is arranged in a checkerboard pattern, and vines have only grown on half. It looks easy to climb.

You're eager to make up for the embarrassment at the back door. "Yeah," you find yourself saying. "Let's do it."

Climb the lattice and *TURN TO PAGE 18*

18

You step up to the lattice and grab the wood, giving it a cautious tug. It seems sturdy enough.

"Be careful," Emma warns.

You take a deep breath and step up into the first opening. Reaching above, you pull yourself one foot into the air. Nothing bad happens. *Hey, this might work!* you think to yourself. You begin to climb in earnest, one hand or foot at a time. It's just like climbing a rock wall at the gym, except for the twisted, curving vines that scrape against your fingers.

"You were right, Emma," you call when you're ten feet off the ground. "It holds my weight just fine."

"The window is to the right a little bit," Emma says. "Move that way some more."

She's right. You follow her directions and move in that direction until you reach the underside of the windowsill. You stop when your head is level with the glass.

"What do you see?" Jake calls.

"The window's too dirty," you say. You turn to look at them–and the balcony to your right catches your eye. Three plants sit in big pots of soil. One of them has something shiny glowing on it, on top of the dirt.

"I... think I see something," you say. "On the balcony."

"Jump!" Jake yells. "See what it is."

It's only two feet to the edge of the balcony, where it would be easy to climb over. Plus, there's a door leading into whatever room is there. Or, you could try opening the window in front of you.

To play it safe and open the window, *TURN TO PAGE 44*

To jump to the balcony, *TURN TO PAGE 31*

"Guys," you say, "we're thinking too hard. Let's just use the front door."

They follow you up the path of broken walking stones and onto the dilapidated porch, carefully avoiding the holes in the wooden steps. Spiderwebs hang in the corners above you, thick and menacing. Next to the door is a window leading into another room. Eager to get inside, you pull out the key and jam it into the lock.

It won't turn!

"What the..." you say, jiggling the handle. "It's locked, and the key doesn't work."

"Why would Mr. Goosen give us a key that doesn't work?" Emma says.

You shrug. "Maybe the key is to a different door?"

"I've got a key right here," Jake says, picking up a broken chunk of brick from the ground. "This window leads into the billiards room."

"Jake!" Emma says. "Put that down. We've looked at the map, there are other ways inside. We don't need to break a window."

"What does it matter?" Jake whines. "The house is going to be bulldozed tomorrow anyways!"

To smash the window, *TURN TO PAGE 23*
To try another entrance, *RUN TO PAGE 32*

20

"I don't think it's safe to go back outside," you say. "Let's look around."

Since Emma is the only one with a light, you're forced to stick together. Huddled in the center of the cellar the three of you slowly rotate around the room, following the cone of light given off by the flashlight. Most of the basement is dusty and filled with junk: a cluster of old rusty bicycles, a mechanical lawn mower, cardboard boxes stacked and crumpling as if they'd gotten wet.

In one corner of the room is an ancient-looking wine rack, filled with old glass bottles in rows and columns. To the left is a small flight of stairs leading to a door inside the house. You're about to suggest that you guys go inside when Jake says, "Check it out!"

Emma swings the light to where he's pointing, over to the right. Two massive crates rest against the wall, the kind you would see packed with straw and priceless archaeological artifacts. From there you can tell the tops are still nailed shut.

To investigate the wine rack, *SHUFFLE TO PAGE 91*

If you'd rather see what's in the crates, *TURN TO PAGE 102*

Alone in that dark, unfamiliar room, fear gets the better of you. You dart toward the open door...

...and trip over your own legs. You fly through the air spectacularly, landing on your elbows and sliding next to the bed.

"Woah buddy, it's just me," Jake says as he jumps down into the room. "Didn't realize you scared so easily."

"I wasn't scared," you say weakly. "I heard a creepy noise." You start to get up but see something under the bed. It looks like a greeting card, but really old.

Reach under the bed and *TURN TO PAGE 22*

22

Dearest Mary,

It feels like only yesterday that you were born. We love you more each day, and always will.

Love, mother and father

January 21

"Mary," you tell the others. "The girl whose room this was was named Mary. Her birthday is January 21."

"Well Mary's stuff is about to get bulldozed," Jake mutters. "Let's look around."

Search the room and *TURN TO PAGE 47*

"Jake's right," you decide. "It's going to be bulldozed tomorrow, you heard Mr. Goosen says so himself. One broken window isn't going to hurt anything."

Emma looks annoyed, but that's all the permission Jake needs. He winds up like he's throwing his best fastball and fires the brick through the window. The glass shatters, blowing shards inward into the room.

"Right down the middle!" Jake exclaims.

You approach the window. The hole is just big enough to reach inside and unlock the window, but as you touch the latch you realize the window was unlocked the whole time. Better not tell Emma that. You pretend to unlock it, then lift the window open with the grinding noise of old wood scraping against old wood.

Your friends look at you expectantly. Apparently you're the one who has to go first. *It's just an old house,* you think to yourself as you step inside the window.

You land on your tip-toes to avoid the glass, but you lose your balance and slip. You throw your hands out to stop your fall, landing like you're doing a push-up. Thankfully you don't hit any glass!

But as you begin to get up, you notice something in the corner of the room, underneath the window. Behind a thin spiderweb is a coin, small and silvery. It has John F. Kennedy on the face, and "LIBERTY" written around the outside.

"Are you okay, Mike?" Emma calls.

To reach for the coin, *TURN TO PAGE 87*
To ignore it, *FLIP TO PAGE 82*

24

You let out a scream as you fall backwards through the hole. The last thing you see is the ceiling rushing away from you as something smashes into your back. The world goes white.

Everything aches: your back and legs and arms. After what feels like an eternity you open your eyes. Even *those* hurt.

"Mike? Mike! Are you okay?"

You see your friends faces staring down at you from very far away. They're still upstairs in the office. They keep yelling your name.

"Errr..." you moan, pushing up on your elbows. "I think... I think I'm okay."

The surface beneath you feels cracked and splintered. You slide off and fall even farther, to more solid ground. As you stand you realize you landed on a grand piano. The cushions resting on its surface broke your fall. Apparently that's the *only* thing it broke, you realize after patting yourself down. The piano is ruined though, smashed in the middle with uncoiled piano wire hanging out of the sides.

"Stay right there," Emma says. "We're coming to get you."

"No way!" Jake cries. "I'm not going down there."

You frown up at them. "What's wrong?"

"Jake thinks he saw a *ghost.*"

"I didn't say it was a ghost," he protests. "It was just a... thing. White and transparent. I swear it flew out of the piano after he smashed it..."

"Sounds like a ghost to me," Emma said. "But I didn't see anything."

You look around the room. There's only one door. You wave at your friends and say, "Guys, it's okay. I'll come back upstairs. Wait for me there."

Exit into the hall *ON PAGE 54*

You feel an inspiring burst of courage. "Move backwards slowly," you hiss at Emma, tightening your grip on the ax handle.

"But..."

"*Do it.*"

Emma obeys, gently pulling a paralyzed Jake with her. The spider swings its head toward them and makes a gargling noise. It steps forward.

You lift the ax with incredible speed, swinging harder than you've ever swung anything in your life. But the spider kicks its leg forward, striking the ax handle and knocking it out of your hands.

That was a really bad idea, you think to yourself. The spider is now completely focused on you. It makes another gargling noise as it leans forward, just a few feet away. You suddenly know what a trapped fly feels like.

Prepare to meet your end *ON PAGE 26*

26

Just before the spider pounces, something strikes it in the face with a hollow *thud*. A bottle clatters to the floor.

The spider makes a high-pitch screeching sound as another bottle hits it, then a third. You stare, dumbfounded.

"What are you waiting for?" Emma cries. "I can't throw bottles at it forever! *RUN.*"

You shake off your senses and spin toward the door. Emma throws a final bottle at the beast–which continues to shriek–before following. The three of you bound up the stairs, throw open the door, and slam it behind you.

You're in a hallway now, with the front door to your left. Before you can examine the area more, Jake sprints around the corner to the right. Not wanting to be left alone, especially since you aren't sure if the spider can get through the door, you follow him down another corridor and through a doorway. As soon as you're through Emma slams the door.

The three of you lean against the wood, panting. "Wow Emma," Jake says after a few moments. "I didn't know you had an arm like that. You could be a baseball pitcher!"

Emma flexes a bicep and puts on a serious face.

You pull out the map, barely visible in the light from the far windows. "I think we're in the den."

Explore the den *ON PAGE 80*

The three of you exit the bedroom. You assumed it was a narrow hallway, but in actuality it's a wide open balcony area overlooking the staircase leading down to the first floor. The balcony is shaped like a square, with rooms running off of it at regular intervals.

You approach the balcony and look down. The stairs are wide and lined with carpet, with ornately-carved wooden railings spiraling down. Although the stairs are intact, the second floor balcony is not: one large section appears broken, as if a giant had smashed it through with a massive fist, leaving a five foot-wide gap.

"How did Mr. Goosen live here?" Emma wonders out loud.

You realize she's right. You've kicked up so much dust from the wooden floors that it now covers your shoes. Cobwebs streak from the banister railing all the way to the ceiling. Even in the semi-darkness the house appears like it's been deserted for decades.

"Want to jump the gap to the other side of the hall?" Jake asks. "It's only a few feet!"

You shake your head. "There's two rooms on this side. Let's check them out first." You can see tile in the first room, which means it's probably a bathroom. You open the second door; it appears to be an office.

To head into the bathroom, *SLIDE OVER TO PAGE 33*
To try the office, *TURN TO PAGE 60*

28

"Just a second!" you yell. The closet looks too appealing to pass up.

You approach slowly, keeping an eye on the glowing light underneath the door. You place your hand on the doorknob and twist it silently, then with a swift motion yank the door open.

At first nothing seems remarkable. There's a rack with four heavy fur coats hanging down, and a few shoe boxes on the floor. What caused the glowing light under the door? Whatever it was, it's gone now.

You're about to leave when one of the fur coats whips back and forth on the rack, knocking the others to the side. It twists on the hanger to face you.

A pale, mist-like apparition is nestled inside the coat. It's a little girl, you realize.

"HELLO!" she cries at you excitedly. She seems to be snuggling inside the woman's coat, though it's much too big for her. "My name's Elizabeth. Do you know my birthday?"

"Your... your birthday?" you stammer.

"Yes! Tell me my birthday." She stares at you expectedly. "Is it January 21, or May 14? Tell me!"

If you think it's January 21, *TURN TO PAGE 30*
If you think it's May 14, *TURN TO PAGE 108*
If you'd rather not play games with a ghost, *RUN TO PAGE 145*

You're not a big fan of Fantasy or Science Fiction. "Let's try random," you say, looking at Emma and Jake for confirmation.

"Random. Okay." The little girl becomes very solemn. "Are you ready?"

The three of you bob your heads.

"What is Ray Bradbury's most famous novel, about a fireman whose job is to burn books?"

Jake laughs out loud. "*Burn* books? Firemen are supposed to put out fires, not start them!"

The ghost girl gives him a blank look. "Hopefully the two of *you* know more than he does," she tells you and Emma.

To answer Slaughterhouse Five, *TURN TO PAGE 76*
To answer The Fireman, *OPEN TO PAGE 137*
To answer Fahrenheit 451, *FLIP TO PAGE 124*

30

"January 21," you say.

"*What?*" she demands. "That's not my birthday. That's my *sister's* birthday!"

Oops.

"I'm... I'm sorry," you stammer. "I got confused. I didn't mean to..."

The girl begins to pout. "You don't care about me," she whines, "do you?"

"I... of course I do!" you say. "I care about you a lot, Elizabeth!"

"No you don't," she says. "You're *lying*. I hate it when people lie."

You take a step back, preparing to make a run for it. But the door closes forcefully behind you, plunging you into darkness.

Uh oh. Find out what happens *ON PAGE 115*

The balcony's not that far. You inch to the edge of the lattice, eying the gap and the drop to the deck below. Jake and Emma look up with wide eyes.

Pushing with your feet, you leap into the air and grab onto the balcony railing.

Your foot slips on the slimy wood, but your grip is strong. You dangle for a moment before pulling yourself up...

There's a sickening *crack*. The wood along the railing snaps free and throws you backwards.

Slam.

The next thing you know, Emma and Jake are staring down at you. "Mike? Mike! Can you hear us?"

You try to sit up but feel very dizzy. The house and your friends and the ground are all spinning in circles. Then you notice the searing pain in your arm.

"Guys, I... I think I broke my arm."

It will only end up being a hair-line fracture, but you're still going to need a cast. You'll be fine in a few weeks, but for now it looks like this is...

THE END

32

"Let's try around the side," you say. You've got a strange feeling about this house, and don't feel sure of yourself, but thankfully your friends follow.

The path between the house and woods is crowded with encroaching tree limbs. You push through them, keeping your head low.

"OW!" shouts Jake. You look back and he's holding his head. The tree limb next to him is swaying. "You hit me!"

"Sorry," you mutter. You'd better be a little more careful!

The path ends at a clearing, where the door to the basement rests against the house at a diagonal angle. The door frame disappears into the ground below.

And a heavy padlock connects the hinge to the frame.

"Aww," Emma says, walking up and grabbing the lock. After examining it she lets go, and it clatters back against the wood with the hollow sound of heavy iron. "I guess we'll try around back?"

"No way," Jake says from a few feet away. He's standing next to a tree stump, where a long wood-chopping ax is lodged. Jake pulls it free, hefting the weight. "Watch this!"

You begin to tell him to wait, but it's too late. He raises the ax high and charges forward.

Jump out of the way *ON PAGE 42*

"Let's go room by room," you decide. "The bathroom's closest, so let's try that first."

They follow you inside. The tile is covered in the same layer of dust, making the floor slippery beneath your feet. A window in the wall lets in a diagonal beam of light, illuminating an array of floating particles. To the left is a sink and toilet, on the right is an antique-looking bathtub with four legs shaped like paws, covered by a curtain in the ceiling.

There's not much to see, and the space is cramped with three. You open the medicine cabinet in the wall but there are just a few old bottles covered in the same dust as everything else. The area beneath the sink is similarly devoid of anything interesting.

You're about to tell your friends to back up when suddenly the toilet flushes.

All of you freeze as you listen to the water swirl and gargle. For a long time nobody makes a sound.

"What...?" Emma whispers.

"I didn't do it," you whisper back. For some reason it feels better to keep your voice low.

The toilet doesn't flush all the way, however. It makes the same noise it makes when it's clogged, with the soft banging of pipes from the water pressure.

And then a *thing* appears. It looks like some sort of green tentacle, flopping over the edge of the toilet bowl.

Everyone screams, even Jake.

The tentacle hangs there and begins moving again. A second one flops over the other side, sticking to the wall.

To get out of there, *RUN TO PAGE 59*
To hide in the bathtub, *DART OVER TO PAGE 15*

34

"Heck if I know," you say. "I feel like we missed something along the way..."

"Well you've indulged your curiosity," Jake says. "Can we grab the *real treasure* now?"

"But..." you say, lowering the scroll. "I bet if we keep trying we can figure this out."

It's no use. Even Emma has her arms crossed, shaking her head.

You sigh. "Fine." You let the scroll drop to the floor and turn back to the safe. You kneel before it, reaching inside.

The safe door screams shut, slamming against your hand. "OW!" you cry, yanking your hand back. "What the..."

The safe fades away, materializing into the ghost of the little girl from before.

And she's very unhappy.

"YOU WERE SUPPOSED TO PLAY WITH ME!" she shrieks. "YOU WERE SUPPOSED TO USE MY SPECIAL CODE!"

Prepare to run *ON PAGE 119*

You reach forward carefully and pluck the tiara between two fingers. A cold sensation washes over you for a moment, but then it's gone.

Watching your step–you don't want to fall *again*–you slide along the wall toward your friends in the middle of the room. "Ta-da!" you say, holding the tiara in your palm reverently.

They ooh and aah at the sight.

Outside the trees are swaying furiously in the wind, scraping against the windows and banging against the wall. The windows are so old that they have cracks in the frame, allowing the wind to howl and whistle.

"Does anyone else feel like an intruder all of a sudden?" Emma asks.

The wind changes tempo and becomes strangely voice-like. "Noooo..." it seems to say, angry and mournful all at the same time. Soon you begin to think it's not just the wind at all. It sounds like a little girl.

You nod. "Let's get out of here."

Head for the front door *ON PAGE 36*

36

The howling follows you out of the office and into the hall. It grows in intensity as you take the stairs two at a time. The wind swirls inside the house, tossing cobwebs and dust into spinning tornado-like pillars. Each of you is hurried along by a shared, unspoken fright, the immediate need to get out of the house as soon as possible.

You reach the bottom of the stairs and cross the entranceway to the front door. You turn the knob and pull...

...and nothing happens! "It won't open!" you yell over the train-like wind.

"Dude!" Jake says. He reaches up and pulls back the deadbolt. Still being pulled by your hands, the door abruptly flies open.

You dash outside, too scared to feel embarrassed.

Something's waiting for you. You skid to a halt and find Mr. Goosen standing on the porch! "Woah now," he says, putting up his hands. His palms seem strangely pale. "What's the rush?"

"The house, there's a..." you begin, but you trail off. The inside of the house behind you is calm and silent, no hint of the maelstrom you had just escaped.

"Such imaginations," Mr. Goosen says. "Ahh, the tiara?" He reaches forward as if to take it but holds back at the last moment.

"You're not going to change your mind," Jake asks suspiciously, "are you?"

"No, of course not. I was just... I had hoped you'd find the... ahh, nevermind." He looks at his gold pocket watch. "Maybe in another life. The princess's tiara is a fine choice."

And just like that Mr. Goosen fades in front of you, like steam above a pot.

"What the..."

"Let's get home," you say, looking at the dark sky. You're not sure what was up with Mr. Goosen, but you've got your treasure, so this is...

THE END

"Fantasy," you select. "Let's do fantasy." Swords and magic always were your favorite!

"Okay," says the girl, lowering her voice even further. A hushed silence falls over the room. "In the Harry Potter book series, what's Harry Potter's middle name?"

If you think it's John, *TURN TO PAGE 76*
If you think it's James, *TURN TO PAGE 124*
If you think it's Jacob, *TURN TO PAGE 137*

38

"Might as well give it a spin," you declare, turning the dial so rapidly that the numbers blur. It makes a buzzing noise like a bumble bee as it rotates over and over. It seems to spin forever before slowing to a stop.

You wrap your fingers around the handle and give it a yank.

The safe opens with a soft *click.*

"Holy cow, guys!" you yell. "It worked!"

But it works *too* well. You let go of the handle but the safe flies open with a *bong,* like some giant gong was rung right next to you. The safe door slams into your knees. You're so surprised by the safe's sudden liveliness that you stumble backwards into the hole in the floor.

TUMBLE TO PAGE 24

"Didn't Mr. Goosen say something outside about something being important..." you mutter.

"Memories!" Emma exclaims. "He said the most important things were memories."

"Well where do we find memories?" Jake said.

Emma laughs out loud and points at his feet. "Right there, dummy!"

The three of you look at the box of old photographs.

"Ohhh!"

You rummage through the box, tossing aside family photographs of Mr. Goosen, his wife, and what must have been their children when they were very young. And at the bottom of the box is something glinting in the dim light...

"A diamond ring!" Emma says, pulling it out. The gem is the size of your thumbnail!

Check out the ring *ON PAGE 99*

40

"I definitely think the riddle refers to a baby," you say. "What else is more precious than that?"

"So...?"

"So we need to check the crib."

Jake and Emma nod, though they don't look too excited about it.

They let you lead the way toward the crib. The wood creaks slightly as the rocker scrapes against the floor. You near the edge of being able to see inside, and pause to gather your courage.

***

Look inside the crib *ON PAGE 85*

Mutant jello? Holy cow!

"Get it away from me!" Jake cries as he scrambles away. "GET IT AWAY!"

You pull him to his feet as the mutant food approaches. It's not very fast, but it's *a mutant piece of food hopping on the ground like a bunny rabbit.* It's time to get the heck out of here.

"This way!" you yell, leading your friends back into the hall.

You cross the house to the side you haven't explored yet. You reach the end of the hall where two doors are open and waiting. The Den is to the left, and the Piano Room to the right.

Before you can make a decision, the jello makes a giant leap forward, landing in the doorway of the Den. Not needing to give directions, the three of you flee into the Piano Room and swiftly close the door.

The door rocks with a soft *splat* as the jelly bounces against it. Even through the door you can smell its terrible stench! But it looks like it cannot pass through the door, and slowly the awful smell fades.

"I guess we're in the Piano Room now," Emma mutters.

Check out the Piano Room *ON PAGE 43*

42

You grab Emma's arm and pull her out of the way as Jake charges forward with the ax over his head, yelling a battle cry like some maniac. With both hands he bring the head down with deadly speed.

And misses.

The ax smashes into the wooden door, half a foot to the left of the padlock. Jake stands there with both hands still on the ax handle, looking genuinely shocked. When he realizes he missed he snarls and begins trying to pull the ax out of the wood.

"Nice swing, Barry Bonds," Emma says.

"It's getting dark! I couldn't see!"

You both chuckle as he struggles to get the ax free. When he does, he takes another–more careful–swing. This time he strikes the padlock perfectly. It splits it down the middle, both halves falling to the side and sliding to the ground. "Okay!" Jake yells.

You and Emma get to your feet as he pulls the doors open with a creak of rusty hinges. Darkness stares back at you. After a moment your eyes adjust and you see a few steps leading down into the basement, but that's all. Everything beyond is pitch black.

There's a noise down by the street, the sound of a barking dog. You lean away from the house and look down the path: Old Mrs. Hollencamp, the neighborhood snoop, is walking her Yorkie down by the street. She's peering in your direction, squinting. You hear her call out, "Who's there?"

"Let's get out of here!" Jake hisses.

"We're allowed to be here," Emma says. "We'll just explain that to Mrs. Hollencamp."

To wait for Mrs. Hollencamp, *TURN TO PAGE 16*
If you want to brave the basement, *JUMP TO PAGE 61*
To head to the back yard, *RUN TO PAGE 63*

The safety of the Piano Room is a welcome relief. Everything in here seems fragile and expensive: a glass table against the wall covered in crystal figures of different exotic animals; the huge oil paintings on the wall of portraits that looks like they're of people from the 1700s; a gold and glass chandelier hanging in the center of the room.

And of course the grand piano in the corner.

It's too magnificent to look at anything else. Its wood is polished to a shiny black, both on the piano itself and the bench in front. The keys are so white they practically glow.

Emma pulls open the bench to look at the music books inside. "Lots of classics here. Bach, Rachmaninoff..."

BONG.

One of the deep piano keys makes a noise.

"Jake, stop messing around."

"It's not me!" he protests. "What if it's one of those pianos that plays on it's own? Like a robot?"

"You mean a player piano?" Emma snorts. "This is *not* one of those."

"I'm telling you, I didn't do it..."

Take a closer look *ON PAGE 51*

44

Your shoulder hurts too much and you're not sure you want to test it by jumping. Instead you reach up and push against the window. It slides open with a creak of wood on wood.

You take a deep breath and pull yourself into the opening, falling onto the floor inside.

The smell of musty dust hits your nose, and it takes your eyes a moment to adjust. There's a four-post bed draped with pink ribbon, with flowery bedspread and ruffled pillows. A small writing desk has an array of colored pencils on it, and a pile of stuffed animals are neatly arranged in the corner. It's very obviously a girl's bedroom, someone younger than a teenager.

A noise whispers from just beside your ear. "Helloooooo..."

You whirl your head around but nothing is there. What was that? "Who's there?" you ask. The dark room remains silent. But you're *certain* you heard something.

Suddenly there's a shuffling noise behind you. The door in front of you is open, with a dark hallway beyond.

Run into the hallway and *TURN TO PAGE 21*
Defend yourself by *TURNING TO PAGE 45*

You're not going to let some spooky noise scare you. You spin around, hand curled into a fist, swinging wildly at the air. A cry of battle escapes your lips.

And you smack your buddy Jake in the arm, right as he's coming through the window.

"Ahh!" he cries, falling to the floor. He gets up and looks like he wants to pummel you. "What'd you do that for?"

Emma follows through the window close behind. "What's wrong?"

"Mike punched me!"

You put your hands up defensively. "I'm sorry! I didn't think it was you."

Jake rubs his arm. "Who else would it be, leather-brain?"

"I... heard something. A noise."

"A noise?" Emma repeats flatly.

"Yeah, it sounded creepy, like..." you trail off as you see the look of disbelief on their faces. It sounds crazy in your head without even saying it out loud. "Nevermind," you say instead. "Let's just look around."

Search the room and *TURN TO PAGE 47*

46

"Science Fiction!" Jake decides before you can say anything. "Ask me about Star Wars. I know more than anyone else in school!"

"Star Wars is a movie," Emma says, rolling her eyes.

"There are books too!"

The ghost floats down to you, her voice barely above a whisper. "Science Fiction. Okay. Are you ready?"

The three of you nod.

"Who is the author of the novel, Dune?"

To answer Frank Herbert, *TURN TO PAGE 124*

To answer Isaac Asimov, *TURN TO PAGE 137*

To answer Robert Heinlein, *GO TO PAGE 76*

Jake opens the closet. Emma checks the writing desk. You walk to her bedside table and open the drawers.

Some pencils, a hair brush, a spindle of yarn. Nothing interesting. An old-style lamp made of brass that used to be much shinier sits on the surface, with a faded yellow lampshade over it. You reach up into it–shivering as you feel spiderwebs–and try turning it on. Nothing happens.

"Aww man, there's just junk in here," Jake calls. "A bunch of little dresses that look like they were worn by someone on the Titanic."

You eye the stack of stuffed animals, but decide not to touch them. You get the distinct impression that they were carefully stacked in a specific fashion. It already feels wrong going through someone else's stuff, even with Mr. Goosen's permission. But somehow disturbing the toys feels taboo. None of them are valuable, anyways.

You say, "Guys, I don't think we're going to find anything–"

"Hey, check this out," Emma interrupts. She's bent over the desk with something in her hands.

See what Emma has and *TURN TO PAGE 88*

48

You're not in the mood for Jake's hijinx. "Come on," you say, ignoring him. "There's nothing in here. Let's try another room."

"Oh come on..." Jake complains.

"Yeah, let's go," Emma agrees.

Jake glumly drops the cue onto the pool table. "Jeez, lighten up. I was just trying to have some fun."

Enter the hallway *ON PAGE 65*

For some reason, you're feeling lucky. "Is your birthday April 2?" you guess, saying the first date that pops into your head.

The ghost girl stares at you, and for a moment you dare to think you were right. Then her face twists angrily. "NO!" she screams. "You don't know my birthday at all!"

The girl disappears back to mist. You're abruptly submerged in darkness as the pantry door slams shut.

You hear the doorknob rattle. "It's locked!" Jake says.

Boxes of food begin falling off the shelves. You cry out as one smashes your toes.

Emma asks, "What do we do?"

To smash the door open, *TURN TO PAGE 114*
If you have the pool cue, *TURN TO PAGE 70*

50

You roll the ivory cube across the ground, scraping away small chunks of dust. With a shudder and a spin it comes to a stop.

"Left window it is," you say.

"If this turns out bad for us..." Emma warns.

"I know, I know," you say.

Emma and Jake stand back as you approach. The glass is faded and frosted from years of disuse. There's definitely no way to peek outside first.

Well, here goes nothing! You grab the bottom of the window and yank.

It doesn't budge.

You pull a second time with no luck. The window is stuck, or the wood is so warped it can no longer move inside the frame. Jake comes over and gives it a try but fares no better.

"Well I guess we're trying the other window," you say.

"Huh," says Emma. "I guess that was one choice that didn't matter."

Jake says, "That's a first!"

Open the right window *ON PAGE 94*

You lean forward to take a closer look at the piano when the keys begin moving on their own. *DUH duh DUH duh DUH duh dih deh.*

Jake glares at Emma. "It's not a player piano," she whispers. "I'm certain."

The same eight notes play again: *DUH duh DUH duh DUH duh dih duh.*

"Hey, that's the beginning of Fur Elise," you say. "It's Beethoven. I know this!"

"I think you're right," Emma says.

The piano plays the same eight notes over again.

"I... I think it wants us to play the next note." You don't know how you know, but you feel certain.

"So what's the next note in Fur Elise?" Jake says.

"It's the 9th note," Emma chips in. They both look at you for the answer.

If it's an A or B, *TURN TO PAGE 57*

If it's a C or D, *FLIP TO PAGE 69*

If it's an E, F, or G, *GO TO PAGE 95*

52

"You're crazy, Emma," you say. "The door is right there, and we have the key!"

"But we don't even know if the key..."

You ignore her and dart to the door. You jam the rusted key inside the keyhole and turn.

It works!

You give Emma a smug look as you turn the knob. The door opens a fraction of an inch before bumping into something on the other side. "Uh oh."

"What's wrong?" Emma asks as you shove against the door.

"It's stuck!"

Jake joins you, but even with both guys throwing their weight the door refuses to budge. The sound of Mrs. Hollencamp's Yorkie draws closer.

"Come on, let's try climbing!" you yell. The three of you run away from the door and arrive at the lattice just as Mrs. Hollencamp rounds the corner. You freeze.

"Ahh ha!" Mrs. Hollencamp says, pointing a wrinkled finger at you. "I knew I heard someone back here." She looks from one face to another. "Now this is quite a surprise. I would have expected this from Jake, but Mike? And *Emma?*"

Emma waits patiently for her to finish. She puts on her most polite voice. "This is a simple misunderstanding. We just spoke to Mr. Goosen, and he said we could go inside his house one last time before it was bulldozed."

"What?" she asks. She looks taken aback by the statement.

"It's true," you say. Jake nods.

The old woman looks angry. "That's not funny. *Not funny at all.* I cannot believe you children you play such a cruel, distasteful joke. Especially so soon after Mr. Goosen..."

"No, it's true!" Emma sputters. "We're not making a joke at all!"

Mrs. Hollencamp reaches forward and grabs your arm. She has a surprising grip for a grandmother. "Come with me. We're going to go explain this to your parents and see what they say!"

She begins to lead you away. Jake looks like he wants to bolt, but then hangs his head and follows with Emma. Maybe you'll be able to explain to your parents what happened, and return before the bulldozers. But for tonight you've reached...

THE END

You feel around on the wall by the door and find a light switch. The closet is suddenly aglow. There are two racks of clothes: suits and business clothes on the right, and dresses and blouses on the left. Underneath are stacks of cardboard boxes, with stacks of shoeboxes on shelves above the racks of clothes.

"Might as well start looking."

Jake opens the first cardboard box he sees, and Emma grabs one of the shoeboxes. You turn to the boxes to your left and begin rummaging through. The first box has nothing but socks in them, neatly folded pairs with their cuffs tucked-in so they stay together. The next box has men's underwear, which you quickly close and push away.

"There are some fancy shoes in here," Emma says. She holds up a pair of tan-colored heels with sparkly straps.

"Nobody cares about shoes," Jake says, his head buried in a box.

"I don't care either! I'm just saying this stuff is expensive."

You go through two more boxes, but it's all clothes. You sigh and look around the closet. The clothes hanging from the racks look interesting. Your dad always leaves money and other stuff in his suit pockets. Maybe there's jewelry attached to the dresses.

Which is it: suits or dresses?

Investigate the dresses ON PAGE 148
Search the suits ON PAGE 143

54

The piano room exits into a main hallway. The stairs are by the front door, so you hang a left in that direction.

A glowing yellow light catches your eye. It's coming from underneath the door of what must be a closet, nestled underneath the staircase. The light is brilliant, shooting across the faded wooden floorboards.

"Mike! Are you coming?" Jake calls from upstairs.

To open the closet, *TURN TO PAGE 28*
To join your friends, *GO TO PAGE 13*

"It's just a little wolf spider," you say. "I don't think we need to–"

"I'm outta here!" Jake blurts out. And with that he grabs the flashlight out of Emma's hands and sprints toward the door leading into the house.

Your options are to follow Jake or stay in complete darkness. Following Jake is an easy choice.

You bound up the stairs and into an entrance hall. It's almost nighttime outside, but there's enough light drifting inside for you to see. To the left is the front door you didn't take. Ahead of you is the billiard room. But you hear Jake to the right, so you quickly dash that way.

The wooden floor changes to tile as you skid to a stop in the kitchen. Jake is bent over, hands on his knees, panting with fright.

"Jeez, Jake... it was just a spider," Emma says with more than a hint of derision.

"Stop fooling around," he scolds. "Let's just look for our treasure and get out of here."

Examine the kitchen *ON PAGE 56*

56

You walk across the kitchen's smooth tile, which is slippery in all the dust. You're conscious of all the footprints you leave behind. When was the last time Mr. Goosen was in his kitchen? Your footprints are the only ones. Something isn't right...

"These cabinets are all empty," Emma says, pointing. She opens a few more and they're all the same. "Huh."

Everything is pretty deserted and boring. There's a pantry behind you with the door closed. "Maybe something is in there," you say.

"Or we could check the refrigerator," Jake suggests. "It sounds like it's still on."

Open the pantry *ON PAGE 103*
To try the fridge, *TURN TO PAGE 58*

"It's A!" you exclaim. To be certain, you play the song in your head a few times. "Yeah. It's definitely A."

Emma nods in agreement as you step forward and press the A key.

BONG.

The ivory keys glow, and the full song begins to play. It sounds so beautiful, the acoustics in the room are fantastic. It sounds like it's not even coming from the piano, but from all around you.

The glowing on the piano keys drifts into the air like mist. It starts to swirl around, forming into a solid shape.

"I don't like this house!" Jake cries.

Find out what it is *ON PAGE 122*

58

"Go ahead," you tell Jake. "See what's in the fridge." You keep your distance, however. If the contents of the fridge are as old as the rest of the house the smell should be *awful.*

Jake pulls it open and immediately covers his nose. "Ugh! It smells like rotten eggs!"

You chuckle, glad that you stayed far away.

"Hey, what's that..." Jake says, leaning forward.

"What is it?" you ask. He's blocking the door so you can't see.

Jake says, "It looks like..."

Without warning, Jake flies backwards as if punched in the chest. He lands on his butt and stares up at the glowing refrigerator opening. Something jumps out of the fridge, making a wet *smack* noise on the ground. As you step to the side to get a better look you see what appears to be a green jello mold, shaped like a cake. It's covered in white mold.

"Jake, why did you grab–"

"I DIDN'T!" he screams. "It jumped out!"

You're about to tell him how crazy that sounds when the jello mold begins hopping forward. Jake scrambles away on his hands and knees.

Mutant jello? *TURN TO PAGE 41*

"Forget this!" you yell. "Let's get out of here!"

Jake and Emma totally agree. They sprint out of the bathroom faster than you do, slipping on the dust-covered floor. The three of you round the corner and slide into the office. Jake is there waiting, and closes the door behind you with a quick, but quiet, motion.

You put your ear against the door, straining to listen.

There's nothing for at least twenty seconds, then the unmistakable sound of something wet, like a flopping fish. You hear it in the hall, growing louder. A shadow passes in front of the doorway.

The doorknob begins to twist.

With a yelp, Emma quickly turns the lock. The thing, whatever it is, rattles the doorknob. You get the impression that it's annoyed. You feel something wet on your feet and realize water is spreading underneath the door!

The thing bumps into the door softly, then harder. You and Jake put your shoulders against the wood, desperate to keep it out. You brace yourself for the next impact.

It never comes. The wet, sliding noise continues as the creature moves away from the door. Eventually it disappears entirely.

"What was *that*?" Emma asks, eyes wide.

"I don't know," you say, "but it's gone now. Let's take a look around."

Examine the office *ON PAGE 60*

60

The office has three wide windows which give plenty of light, although you can tell that night is quickly falling. There's an enormous mahogany wooden desk on the left, the kind that's *really* expensive and probably weighs more than a piano. Papers are scattered over the surface, but there's no computer. A bunch of boxes are stacked to the right, and beyond that is a corner with part of the floor missing. It looks like there's another box over there, just past the huge hole. You flick the light switch on the wall but of course nothing happens.

Jake and Emma are already checking out the desk, so you walk over to the stacks of boxes. They're plain cardboard, bent and warped on the side like they've gotten wet over the years. There's no lettering on the side or any other indication as to what's inside.

You pull the first box off the stack and open the folded top. Although the outside is dusty and mildewy, the inside is pristine. Stacks of photographs inside glass frames stare back at you. Each frame is unique, with a different style brass or silver cover wrought into fancy designs. You pick up the first picture and hold it up into the light. It's black-and-white, cracked and worn around the edges where it meets the frame. It's a family portrait: mother, father, daughter. They're standing in front of what looks like a door.

You put it down on the ground and take a few more out, all similarly aged. A little girl playing the piano while her father smiles. A woman standing in the kitchen, holding a pot and wooden spoon. A man and four of his friends standing around a pool table. For some reason the photos make you sad.

"Hey, is that a *safe?*" Jake blurts out.

See what Jake's talking about on *PAGE 77*

It may be a foreboding sight, but you're not afraid of the dark. "Come on!" you yell, before descending into the cellar.

You take maybe four or five steps before slowing to a stop. Already you can barely see behind you in the soup-like blackness. How can it possibly be so dark? The door was just behind you, yet now it seems a thousand feet away!

One of your friends closes the door, the light closing shut. Now it seems worse.

"Mike?" Emma whispers. You call back to her and her hands touch your arm as she feels around randomly. She grabs your hand and holds it in hers. You can feel her fingers trembling.

A moment later Jake touches you. Content to not move, the three of you remain frozen in place as you listen.

You wait for what seems like hours but hear nothing outside.

A light unexpectedly shines on your face, painfully bright after so much darkness. You shield your eyes and cry out, and the assailant points the light at the ground.

It's Emma, holding the flashlight. "Sorry," she says.

"Why do you have a flashlight?"

"I went to school early this morning to look for worms in the field with Mr. Hanney, the biology teacher. The worms only come out in the dark."

Jake snorts as if that's funny. He's still holding the ax in both hands. He must have left his glove and baseball outside.

"Okay, now what?" Emma asks.

Explore the basement *ON PAGE 20*

62

You crouch down in front of the safe. The dial is a shiny metal compared to the black safe surface. Numbers are etched all around the circle. But what's the combination?

If you know the little girl's birthday, *TURN TO THAT PAGE* (ex. March 10 would be 3-1-0, or page 310)

If you know some other number, *TURN TO THAT PAGE*

If you don't have a clue, spin the dial randomly and *TURN TO PAGE 38*

You hesitate too long, and without warning Jake bolts for the back yard. Your flight instinct kicks in and you yell "Hey, wait up!" as you chase him. Emma protests but soon you hear her follow too.

The lawn–which looks like it hasn't been mowed since before lawnmowers were invented–is brown and cracked. A round patio table with a glass top and a hole in the middle for an umbrella stands surrounded by the grass. Two of the chairs are turned over. A long deck runs along the entire length of the house, with a single set of steps and a door leading inside.

Jake bounds the steps and skids to a halt by the door. You stop next to him, panting. "Should we try the back door?"

"Hey, check this out!" Emma calls. She's up against the wall on the deck. There's a thick wooden lattice nailed against the house, spanning the entire wall from the ground to the second floor. It's covered in vines. "Let's climb this to the second floor."

You wonder where her bad girl streak had come from. "But the door..."

"If we go in the door she'll just follow us."

You hear her Yorkie barking on the side of the house. If you try climbing the lattice it will be close.

To take the safe way inside, open the back door *ON PAGE 52*
If you're feeling dangerous, *CLIMB TO PAGE 100*

64

You look at your friends. "Do you guys know much about literature?"

Jake shakes his head.

"Not enough to play a game!" Emma says.

That decides it for you. The three of you turn and bolt out of the room. "Wait!" the ghost calls behind you. "Don't you want to hear about the Oxford Commaaaaaaaaaa..."

You're in the hallway now. Which way should you go?

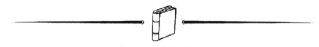

To run across into the Piano Room, *GO TO PAGE 43*

To try your luck upstairs, *TURN TO PAGE 133*

Without any windows, the hallway is darker than the billiards room. It splits off in two directions. A long, thin rug covers the floor, at least thirty feet long.

Emma pulls out the map, squinting in the darkness. "To the left is the Kitchen. Or we can go over to the Den."

"What's a Den?" Jake asks.

Emma says, "You don't know what a Den is? It has a fireplace, and couches and chairs..."

"You mean a living room?"

"It's the same thing, yeah."

"Why don't they just call it a living room?" Jake says.

"It's just an older name..." Emma explains.

You tune them out as you look to the left and the right. Which way should you go?

To head to the Kitchen, *GO TO PAGE 56*
To explore the Den, *TURN TO PAGE 78*

66

"This one's easy," you say. "Samuel Clemens."

"Bingo!" exclaims the little girl. "You guys are smart. I knew you'd be smart."

You and Jake high-five. For once things seem to be going your way in this crazy, creepy house.

"Now for the third and final question," the girl says, voice growing hushed and serious. "For this one you get to choose the topic. Do you want your question to be about Fantasy, Science Fiction, or random?"

To pick Fantasy, *WAVE YOUR WAND OVER PAGE 37*

To pick Science Fiction, *TELEPORT TO PAGE 46*

To pick something random, *READ PAGE 29*

You meet them in the office. Jake is going through a box of photographs. Taking a moment to catch your breath, you tell them what just happened.

"I told you I saw a ghost earlier!" Jake says, looking vindicated.

"So what does it mean?" Emma asks. "'The path to what you THINK is most precious, is underneath what is TRULY most precious.' Such a strange riddle."

"Don't look at me," Jake says. "You're the one who always liked riddle books, Mike."

If you think the answer is there in the Office, *GO TO PAGE 39*
If you want to try to Master Bedroom, *TURN TO PAGE 113*
If you think the clue refers to the Nursery, *TURN TO PAGE 98*

68

Night is falling, so it's now extremely difficult to see. You lean one foot out the window until you feel the balcony with your toes. Then you duck through, stepping down with your other foot. Thunder rumbles in the distance.

Now you're on the balcony with a row of six potted plants.

"Is the prize in one of those?" Emma asks.

"Yeah," Jake said, "but if so, which one?"

You look at the six plants and something tickles your memory. "I've seen this balcony before. When I climbed the vine lattice to get into the little girl's bedroom."

"Ohh yeah," Jake says. I knew it looked familiar!"

"I saw something in one of the pots." You look to the side of the house, trying to re-imagine your vantage. "It was this pot here. The one on the end." Sticking out of the soil is the remains of a sunflower, but now it's brown and dead. The soil still looks fresh and black.

"Reach inside and find out," Jake urges.

"That's easy to say when it's not your hand doing the reaching!"

To dig around in the soil, *FLIP TO PAGE 89*

If you'd rather look around some more, *GO TO PAGE 97*

"I think it's a C," you say. "Yeah, I'm pretty sure."

"Pretty sure?" Jake asks.

"Do *you* have a better idea?" you demand.

"Hey, I'm not the one taking piano lessons."

Emma says, "I think you're right, Mike. Your guess is as good as mine."

You step forward and find the correct octave. Your finger hovers over the C key for a few seconds before finally pressing down.

BONG.

The sound rings out, and you immediately know that it's wrong. "Uh oh," you say.

Jake throws up his hands. "Mike! I thought you said you knew!"

"I'm sorry!"

"Guys, something is happening..." Emma whispers.

Prepare yourself *ON PAGE 140*

THE HOUSE ON HOLLOW HILL

70

You heft the pool cue. "I knew I kept this for a reason," you say, wedging it between the door and the frame like a crowbar.

You lean on the stick but the door doesn't budge. A box of what sounds like cereal hits you in the back. Other bags of food smash open on the ground, spilling their contents across the floor.

Why won't it budge! You groan as you strain against it, and then you feel Jake's hands joining yours on the pool cue. With your combined strength the door pops open and you fall forward into the brighter kitchen.

Food continues flying out of the pantry, so you scramble to your feet. "Let's get out of here!" Jake says. None of you argue. You dash back into the hallway, turning randomly this way and that.

Run into the Den ON PAGE 71

You, Emma, and Jake all stand motionless in the Den, listening. The only sound is your breathing, and your heartbeat pounding in your ears. "I think we're okay," you say.

"I am *not* okay," Jake says. All the blood has drained out of his face. Frankly, he looks like he's seen a ghost.

"Maybe we should leave," Emma suggests. "We could just get out of here, and tell Mr. Goosen what we saw..."

"No way," Jake says. "Nobody will believe us. Besides, I came here for *treasure*. I don't want to leave empty handed."

Explore the Den *ON PAGE 80*

72

"I've got a good feeling about the second crate," you say. "Jake, have at it."

Jake wedges the ax head in between the top of the crate and the side. He pushes up and down on the handle until slowly, one millimeter at a time, the nails begin to loosen. With one final push the entire cover pops off and clatters to the ground, sending a puff of dust into the air all around you.

Coughing and waving your head over your face, you lean over the crate. Jake and Emma join you, all peering inside. The dust begins to fade and the contents come into view.

Three enormous eggs sit inside the crate, resting gently on mounds of straw. They appear cream colored in the light, smooth and shiny as if they're slightly damp.

"Dragon eggs?" Emma whispers, awestruck.

You notice more printed letters on the inside of the crate:

O - S - T - R - I - C - H - E - G - G - S

"Ostrich eggs!" you say. Emma seems disappointed, but you're excited. You pick one up with careful hands and hold it up for them to see.

A voice calls out in the darkness: "Not just any ostrich eggs!"

You nearly jump out of your shoes until you recognize Mr. Goosen gliding toward you.

"You scared the skin off us!" Emma says. "How did you get in here? We didn't see any doors open."

He ignores the question. His eyes are transfixed on the egg. "We had to call them ostrich eggs to get them through customs. These are millions of years old, from the Jurassic era!"

"Dinosaurs!" Emma cries.

But then Mr. Goosen is gone as quickly as he had arrived. "That was creepy," Jake says. "And he looked weird, too. Like I could almost see through him, like a..."

Across the cellar, the door to the outside swings open. It seems like there's a storm brewing. "We'd better get out of here."

As you walk home you aren't sure whether to keep the egg or donate it to a museum. But what you are sure of is that this is...

THE END

74

"...like spiderwebs," Emma finishes. A shadow descends over the thick spiderwebs, pushing them aside.

The beast emerges from the hole, pulling itself out by its eight hairy legs. It pauses between the wine racks, looking at the three of you with its multi-faceted eyes. It seems to focus on you, which is when you remember that you're still holding the ax with the spider guts all over it.

"We've made a huge mistake," you say.

Jake whimpers.

The spider sets itself down on the floor. It towers over you. Saliva–or venon–drips from its fangs, and its green and yellow body tenses menacingly. As if it's preparing to strike.

You stand very still, speaking out of the side of your mouth. "Guys. What do we do?"

Jake whimpers some more.

"You're the one with the ax!" Emma whispers. "Or would you rather run?"

Run away *ON PAGE 79*
To use your ax, *TURN TO PAGE 25*

76

Books begin flying off the shelves, shooting toward you like cannonballs. "Why don't you know the right answer?" she cries, forlorn. "WHY?"

"I'm sorry!" you yell, but she doesn't hear it over the sound of her own wailing.

Emma grabs your arm. "Let's get out of here!"

The books continue pummeling your backs as you sprint out of the Den and into the hallway. "Quick, upstairs!" you point.

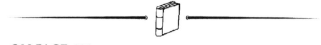

Flee upstairs *ON PAGE 133*

Jake's pointing at the corner with the hole in the floor and the box beyond. But as you draw near and squint in the low light you realize it's not a box at all. The exterior is black matte, and one of the sides is open. A door, with a silver dial on it.

"Hey, I think you're right," you say.

The three of you approach the edge of the big hole. You can see through the jagged wooden floor into the room below. It looks like there's a piano down there.

"There's a small path next to the wall," Jake says, pointing. "You should be able to reach the safe if you hug the wall."

"Why do I have to go?" you ask.

"You know I'm afraid of heights," Jake replies. "I won't even go into my brother's tree house!"

You press your back against the wall and slide down the narrow walkway next to the edge. It's an awfully long fall into the room below. You raise your eyes to the safe to keep yourself from feeling scared. The door is definitely open, and something inside is *glowing!*

You approach the end where the safe sits. The glowing increases. You extend your hand...

...and the safe suddenly slams shut with a *bang.*

"Woah," you say, nearly losing your balance. You teeter before getting your footing.

Your friends stare across the hole at you. "The wind?" Emma asks.

You glance at the windows. They're closed. You'd better not point that out, though.

Examine the safe *ON PAGE 62*

78

"Let's try the Den," you say, interrupting your friends. Emma nods vigorously, happy to stop her argument with Jake.

You turn and walk down the hallway. At the end is an intersection: to the right is the front door, and straight ahead is the door leading down into the cellar. You hear a weird, gargling noise.

"What's *that?*" Jake asks.

"I don't know, but I'm glad we didn't go down there," Emma says.

The Den is around the corner. You pass through an ornate looking doorway and enter the room, closing the door softly behind you.

Explore the Den *ON PAGE 80*

You are *not* about to fight some giant mutant spider. "On the count of three, make a break for the door," you hiss to your friends. Out of the corner of your eye you see Emma nod.

The spider stares at you, waiting. You're unable to look away. You can feel your heart pounding in your chest in the dank, dark cellar.

"One, two... THREE!"

Emma and you scramble away, pushing a paralyzed Jake with you. The flashlight bounces up and down as Emma pumps her arms, alternately illuminating the floor, wall, and ceiling. It's not far to the door. You're halfway there, and can't hear anything behind you, though you're breathing awfully loud.

Emma reaches the steps. Jake follows. You're there, about to jump to safety...

...when something grabs the back of your shoe, tripping you.

You fly forward onto your face. You turn and see a long strand of spiderweb stuck to your shoe. Using your other foot, you push your sneaker off.

Suddenly the spider appears from the darkness. More webbing appears out of nowhere, wrapping around your ankle. The beast reaches forward with a long leg and begins to pull you backwards.

You cry out, but your friends are nowhere to be seen. The open doorway is just out of reach, taunting you with its safety. Strangely, in your moment of fear, you worry that your mother will be angry at you for not practicing the piano. *That's a stupid thing to think about,* you realize, as your dragged backwards into...

THE END

80

Despite its dusty and unused state, the Den has a warm, friendly feel to it. Two brown leather couches face a large brick fireplace. On either side of the fireplace are shelves filled with books, from floor to ceiling. The windows along the wall give a view of the back yard, and let in plenty of light. Dust particles float in the air.

"Look at all the books!" Emma exclaims. The picks up the first one she sees, a thick copy of *The Old Man and The Sea*. She blows off the dust and looks inside. "We have to read this in English class. I bet Mr. Arrieta would love to see a copy this old!"

"Careful," you say. "We're only allowed to take one item, remember?"

"Oh, yeah," she says, swiftly placing the book back in its slot.

In addition to the books, the shelves hold an assortment of special items every few feet. One looks like a porcelain egg on a display stand. Above your head is one of those Russian nesting dolls, with smaller and smaller dolls inside. To the left is a huge sheep horn, ribbed and shaped like the letter U.

"Hey guys, look at this," Jake calls from across the room.

See what Jake has *ON PAGE 81*

He's standing over the coffee table, pointing. As you approach you see a small wooden box, ornately designed. Unlike the table and furniture, there's not a speck of dust on it.

Jake reaches forward. "Don't pick it up!" you say. "We don't know if it's what we want to take."

"I'm just going to open it," Jake says defensively. "Cool your grill."

With a careful hand he opens the lid to the box.

Something white streaks across your vision, flying into the air. With horror you realize it's a little girl, but you can see the ceiling through her body.

"Hi there!" she calls in a hollow voice. "Have you met my sister yet?"

You take a frightened step back. "Hey wait," she says. "I just want to play a game! Don't you want to play a game?"

"What... what kind of game?" Emma stammers.

"A book game!" she says excitedly. "I'll give you a clue, and you have to guess what book it is! You guys *read*, don't you?"

To play her game, *TURN TO PAGE 147*
If you don't know much about books, *GO TO PAGE 64*

82

Mr. Goosen was very specific about what you were allowed to take, and you're not sure if a 50-cent piece would count as the one item of treasure. It's probably best to leave it.

You get to your feet and help Emma and Jake climb through the window into the billiard room.

Now that you're no longer distracted, your other senses awaken. The smell of mold and mildew is thick in the room. A billiard table sits in the center with a thick layer of dust on its surface. A rack of cues is mounted on the wall to the left. On the right is a shelf of empty bottles, with a countertop and three stools underneath.

"Cool!" Jake says, running over to grab a pool cue from the wall. "My uncle has a pool table, but it's nothing like this."

Emma pays no attention to him. "It looks like nobody has been in here in years," she says. "How could Mr. Goosen live like this?"

She's right: there's so much dust and spiderwebs that it's obvious nobody has been in the room in a long time. Is the rest of the house so decrepit? A tingle runs down your spine.

Shake it off *ON PAGE 83*

Jake is examining the pool table, so you walk over to the countertop with the stools. The bottles on the wall behind are molded into cool, unique shapes: one is almost like a pyramid, another is sphere-shaped with a flat bottom and a thin neck sticking out the top. They're all empty, and covered with the same layer of dust as everything else.

Behind the counter are cabinets filled with drinking glasses of all different shapes and sizes. You only look for a few seconds. There's clearly nothing valuable there.

"Hey Mike, do you think I can sink the 8-ball?" Jake asks. He's leaning over the pool table, aiming his cue.

To dare him to try, *TURN TO PAGE 84*
If you'd rather search another room, *GO TO PAGE 48*
To take the stick from Jake, *TURN TO PAGE 93*

"I've seen you play pool before," you taunt. "I bet you a dollar you can't sink it from there."

"You're on!"

Jake leans over the table, resting his elbows on the railing. The cue ball is in the middle of the table, but the 8-ball is at the other end near the corner pocket. He takes his time lining up the shot, smoothly moving the cue back and forth between his fingers. Finally he shoots.

The cue ball rolls across the felt surface, leaving a dust-less trail behind. With a crack of ivory on ivory it strikes the 8-ball, knocking it gently into the corner pocket.

"Booya!" Jake cries, jumping up and pumping his fist. He points at you. "You owe me a—"

He cuts off as a moaning sound fills the room. It seems to come from everywhere and nowhere, all at once. "What's going on?" Emma asks, voice cracking with fright.

"I don't know!"

The pool table begins to shake. Inexplicably, pool balls begin floating out of the pockets. They rise into the air and begin swirling around, like a model of the solar system. You feel paralyzed as they spin around, faster and faster. Suddenly the moaning turns into an angry cry: "*I HATE WHEN FATHER PLAYS POOL.*"

Emma screams.

The sound unfreezes you. Grabbing Emma's hand, you make a run for the door.

Run for your life! *TURN TO PAGE 110*

There's a bundle inside the crib, barely visible in the shadows. Banishing all fear you take the final step forward and lean inside.

At first you think it's a baby. It's bundled that way, wrapped in a blue blanket like a burrito. But the rocking of the crib causes it to roll, and you see shiny, plastic eyes look back at you. "A doll," you say. "It's just a doll."

That gives your friends the signal that it's safe to come closer. They lean inside and then nod. "I think so!"

You all stare at the doll for a long time.

"So... what now?" Jake asks.

"I guess we should pick it up? If what we're looking for is underneath?"

"*I'm* not going to pick it up," he says.

Emma looks no braver.

With a sigh you lean forward. "Why do I have to do everything in this crazy house?"

Pick up the doll *ON PAGE 112*

86

"Pride and Prejudice?" you guess.

The little girl looks shocked. "How could you get that one wrong? It's easy! That's one of the most famous opening lines in literature!"

She starts moaning, and a sudden wind picks up in the room despite the windows being closed. "Guys, I think we're in trouble..."

Suffer the girl's wrath *ON PAGE 76*

You're not about to let a 50-cent piece go to waste. Cringing at the spiderweb, you reach underneath and slide the coin out. It feels heavy in your hands, more than most coins. The mint date is 1964.

"Hey guys," you say as you get to your feet, "check out what I found!"

But as you reappear in the window you see that your friends are no longer alone. "Oh hello there, Michael!" Mr. Goosen exclaims. He's standing on the porch with Emma and Jake.

"Hey Mr. Goosen," you say. You feel strange standing in his house while he's outside. "Hey, uhh... we're sorry for smashing your window. The key..."

"Oh that's quite alright," he says with a wave of a hand. He puts his thumbs through his suspender straps. "Doesn't matter since it's going to be bulldozed tomorrow anyways."

Jake gives Emma an *I told you so* look.

Mr. Goosen's eyes narrow. "However... it appears you've found your treasure already. My, that was fast!"

"This?" you say, glancing at the coin. "It's just a half-dollar. It was sitting in the corner..."

Mr. Goosen wags a finger at you. "I said you could take one item of special value from the house. I was quite specific! And that 50-cent piece is worth about $10 today. It's from 1964."

Jake looks crestfallen. "But... you mean..."

"I'm afraid so," Mr. Goosen nods. "Come on now, let's get you home." He gestures and you sullenly climb back out the window.

A 50-cent piece is better than nothing, but you can't help but wonder what you *could* have found inside the house. Your imagination runs wild as you try to forget that this is...

THE END

88

You look over Emma's shoulder and see a small book open on the desk. "What is it, a book of fairy tales?" Jake says.

"Not a book. A *diary*." She picks it up and shows it off. It's about as thick as your thumb, with one of those metal clasps that closes around the side so it can be locked with a key. "Most of the pages were too faded to read, but this one's as clear as day."

She opens back to the original page and holds it up so you can read:

Today in arithmetic lecture, Elizabeth and I invented a secret language! The code is to take a normal word and shift every letter forward by 3. So the word 'apple' becomes 'dssoh'. We've sent a dozen notes back and forth and none of the other students can read them. They look at us like we are brilliant. Exw uhdoob, lw'v qrw wkdw kdug!

"*But really, it's not that hard!*" you translate. You smile at the others. "I had a secret language like that when I was a kid."

"Big deal," Jake says. "It's already late, and we're losing daylight. Pretty soon we won't be able to see much in here at all. Come on, I want to find something cool!"

You look to the window and see that he's right. You only have about an hour before the sun goes down. "Okay," you say, "let's go check out the hallway."

Lead your friends into the hall *ON PAGE 27*

You're certain you saw something glowing in this potted plant. It's gotta be cooler than the tiara! You can't turn back empty handed.

"Okay," you announce, leaning forward. You slide your fingers into the soil.

It's definitely fresh soil, black and damp. Someone has been keeping up with the house, though apparently only on this single balcony.

"Do you feel anything?" Emma asks.

"I don't think so," you say. You move your hand back and forth in the pot, wiggling your fingers. "I'm not sure there's–"

Your fingers touch something solid.

"I've got something!" you say. It seems to be falling farther in the pot, so you wrap your fingers around it. "It feels cold, like metal."

"Like gold?" Jake breathes. Your friends crowd the window, waiting.

Find out what it is *ON PAGE 90*

90

The coldness feels strange, though. Not quite right. After a few moments you realize why.

"It's not cold," you say. "It's wet. Almost... slimy."

Feeling unnerved, you begin to pull your hand out. But the object seems stuck to your hand.

Oh no.

You yank back on your hand but it hardly budges. With groan of terror you realize that you didn't grab the object. The object grabbed *you*.

"Ahh!"

You cry out but there's little use. Desperately you pull your hand into the air, lifting the entire pot. It's still attached to your hand, spraying soil all over the tiny balcony. With a frantic heave you throw your hand against the railing. The pot smashes open in an explosion of clay and dirt. Something flops onto the balcony floor. You realize that your hand is free!

"What the..." Jake says.

"Ewwwww!" Emma squeals.

The object on the ground looks vaguely like a snake, but fatter. It's like a giant earthworm, but as big as a football. It's covered in tiny spines. You stare at it, frozen in place.

A burning sensation on your hand breaks your paralysis. One of the spines has pierced your palm. There's no blood, but your hand is covered in a reddish rash.

And the rash is spreading.

It moves up your arm with frightening speed. You begin to scream. Rashes aren't deadly, right? They only itch? Will you have to cover it in lotion like poison ivy? These are the questions that run through your mind as you accept that you've hit...

THE END

Emma decides for you by running forward. "My mom collects old wine," she says. "Some of her bottles are over fifty years old!"

Rather than stay in the darkness you follow her over to the wine racks.

The wooden racks are set into the wall, with wine bottle slots spaced about every foot apart. There are eight rows, you count. Dust covers everything; it's impossible to read the bottles without touching them.

Emma does just that, grabbing the first one she sees. The dust cascades off it like a wave as she clears it with a puff of breath. "*Chateau Rousseau, 1988,*" she reads.

Jake picks up a bottle, and something black falls onto the floor. Emma swings the light toward it. A wolf spider, the size of your hand!

"Ahh!" Jake yelps.

"It's just a spider," Emma says.

"I hate spiders!" He shoves the ax into your hands. "Mike, kill it!"

You heft the ax and look down at the little guy. He's not moving, just looking up at you with his eyes shining in the glow of the flashlight.

To kill the spider, *GO TO PAGE 92*

If you'd rather leave it alone, *GO TO PAGE 55*

92

You have no love for spiders. Turning the ax sideways, you bring the flat end of the head down with a loud *clang*. Spider guts shoot out in all directions underneath.

"Ewww."

"Thanks pal," Jake says. It was such a small, easy thing to do, but he seems genuinely grateful. "Let's check out those crates now, okay?"

"But I'm not done looking at these," Emma complains.

"Then you can stay here," Jake says, "while we check out the cool stuff."

Emma says, "I'm the one with the flashlight, dorkus."

As you watch Jake and Emma argue, you feel a low trembling in the ground. It slowly grows more intense, like a train drawing closer. "Uhh, guys?" you say. "Guys? Hello? Do you hear that?"

"Hear wha–" Emma cuts off. She tenses. "What *is* that?"

The vibration is so violent that dust and mortar are shaking off the ceiling. The wine bottles move around, clinking together. "I think it's coming from... *behind* the wine rack."

There's a gap between two of the wine racks, and Emma points the flashlight there. You see a hole in the cement wall as big as a beach ball. You can't see very far inside because it's covered with some whitish, sticky substance.

"Uh oh," Emma says. "That looks like..."

Find out *ON PAGE 74*

You approach Jake and take the cue out of his hand. "Stop playing around. We're here to find treasure, remember?"

"Oh yeah," Jake says, as if he *had* forgotten that.

It feels good to have something in your hand, like a weapon. You heft the cue like a battle-ax.

"Are you scared?" Jake chides.

"I dunno. Maybe."

"You can leave if you want, Mike..."

Emma steps between you two. "You guys are being dumb. Let's go check another room."

You nod at her, but as you leave the room you take the pool cue with you anyways.

Enter the hallway *ON PAGE 65*

94

So it looks like the right window is the one. Cautiously, you approach it and give it a tug.

With the screech of wood on wood in inches upward. You have to wiggle it back and forth in the frame but slowly it moves up. Jake comes over and crouches below the window, pushing it up from underneath. With one final *snap* as part of the frame breaks, the window slides the rest of the way open.

"Good thing it's being bulldozed," Jake mutters, wiping the dust from his hands.

The window leads out to a small balcony, the kind that's meant to hold a few potted plants but not large enough for people to walk around on comfortably. A row of such plants lines the railing. There's enough room for one person, although it would be cramped.

You look at your friends and give a big shrug. "Who am I to argue with a decrypted secret message, found in a safe, whose code we acquired from a creepy moving crib, which we found by solving a ghost's riddle?"

"If you can't trust that," Emma said, "who *can* you trust?"

Do it! Climb onto the balcony *ON PAGE 68*

"I think it's an E," you say. "Yeah, I'm pretty sure."

"Pretty sure?" Jake asks.

"Do *you* have a better idea?" you demand.

"Hey, I'm not the one taking piano lessons."

Emma says, "Mike, I'm not sure. I think it's an F."

Jake throws up his hands. "Neither of you us sure?"

"What do you think it is, then?" You gesture at the piano. "Go ahead. We're all ears."

Jake snickers. "Well I might as well guess, since that's just as good as trusting either of you!"

"Calm down..." Emma begins.

"We've seen enough craziness in this house, I don't want anything more to happen! And I know if you choose the wrong one something is going to happen!"

You're sick of arguing. Trusting Emma, you step forward and press the F key.

BONG.

The sound rings out, and you immediately know that it's wrong. "Uh oh," you say.

"I KNEW IT!" yells Jake angrily.

"Something is happening..." Emma whispers.

Prepare yourself *ON PAGE 140*

96

"I bet the first one says 'TREASURE'," you say. "Let's open that one."

Jake wedges the ax head in between the top of the crate and the side. He pushes up and down on the handle until slowly, one millimeter at a time, the nails begin to loosen. With one final push the entire cover pops off and clatters to the ground, sending a puff of dust into the air all around you. The ax falls inside the crate and the sound of shattering glass rips the air.

"Oh no!" Jake cries.

Coughing and waving your head over your face, you lean over the crate. Jake and Emma join you, all peering inside. The dust begins to fade and the contents come into view.

Three cylindrical cannisters rest inside the crate, suspended in straw. They're made almost entire of glass, showing a glowing green liquid inside.

A fourth cannister is in pieces, the ax head penetrating through the center.

And the green liquid has spilled out. It makes a hissing sound as it drips down through the straw. That's when you notice more letters printed on the inside wall of the crate:

C - H - E - M - I - C - A - L
T - R - E - A - T - M - E - N - T

"Guys," you say, "I think we've made a mistake."

A greenish mist rises up from the crate. Within seconds it's all around you, filling the cellar. You feel a tingling sensation on the skin of your hands and neck. Your eyes begin to sting as you cough and cough.

You fall to your knees, wondering what would have happened if you had gone around to the back yard. You'll never know, though, because unfortunately this is...

THE END

"Something doesn't seem right," you say. "I don't think this is the ultimate treasure."

"Then what is?" Jake asks. "Dude, you gave up a tiara to try this way!"

Emma giggles. "You seem awfully concerned with women's jewelry."

"It's worth a lot! Maybe millions!"

While your friends argue, you begin looking around the balcony. Besides the pots and plants whipping in the growing wind, there's just nothing there. On the other side of the railing is the vine lattice you climbed earlier, and the window into the girl's room. But that's it. Just the balcony and the vines. The vines are overgrown, spilling across the wall. They're *everywhere*, even surrounding the window. How are they attaching to the house? It doesn't really make any sense. In fact, the only way they could–

Suddenly you realize. You reach our and push aside some of the thick vines. The entire wall here is made of that criss-cross wooden lattice!

You look up.

The lattice extends above you, to a small round shape underneath the roof peak. There's a flicker of light and you realize it's a window.

You're not on the top floor. There's an attic above you!

"Guys," you say, "I think I know where it is."

Climb up to the attic *ON PAGE 107*

98

"Babies are awfully precious," you decide. "Let's investigate the nursery."

You tip-toe down the hall and enter the small room adjacent to the Master Bedroom. There's not much to it: a dresser that doubles as a changing table hugs one wall, with an old fashioned pink piggy bank on top. On the opposite wall is a crib.

And the crib is moving.

You don't notice it at first, the movement is so subtle. But then you realize it's gently rocking back and forth, as if by some invisible hand. You share a look with Emma and Jake.

"I'm not sure I want to go near the crib," you say.

"We could always check the piggy bank?" Emma suggests.

To go to the piggy bank, *TURN TO PAGE 106*

To approach the crib, *GO TO PAGE 40*

"Oops," says Mr. Goosen, striding into the office. "I *did* say memories were the most important thing, didn't I? Ahh, I didn't mean for my little girl to confuse you..."

"Your little girl?" you ask.

"Yes, Elizabeth's clue was good but I'm afraid it was misleading. That's my fault. Ahh well, it's too late now. Unfortunately you chose the wrong room. There's no prize in that box."

"But the ring..." Emma says.

"Costume jewelry," he says cheerfully. "There *are* gems in this house, though you three just barely missed them. What you hold is merely plastic."

"Aww," Emma says.

"However," Mr. Goosen says, holding up a finger, "I did say you could only take one item. And seeing as though you've chosen that plastic ring..."

"Oh man!" Jake cries. "Not fair!"

"I suppose some other children will have to come along and finish the job here," he says. "Time to run along now, it looks like a storm is brewing outside."

You run home just as it starts to rain. Jake and Emma argue over the plastic ring–and whose fault it was for taking it–but you still think about the sad little ghost. Maybe you'll know someday, but today is...

THE END

100

You step up to the lattice and grab the wood, giving it a cautious tug. It seems sturdy enough.

"Hurry up!" Emma cries.

You take a deep breath and step up into the first opening. Reaching above you, you pull yourself one foot into the air. Nothing bad happens. *Hey, this might work!* you think to yourself. You begin to climb in earnest, one hand or foot at a time. It's just like climbing a rock wall at the gym, except for the twisted, curving vines that scrape against your fingers. You pick up speed, rushed by the sound of Mrs. Hollencamp's Yorkie on the side of the house, evidence that she draws near.

As you near the top you see a balcony to your right. There's a flowerpot with something shiny on it. Stopping for just a breath, you squint in its direction.

"What are you waiting for?" Emma demands. She's right below your feet on the lattice.

You continue climbing, reaching the window. Not wanting Emma to scold you again, you swiftly open the window and jump into the dark room.

Hide *ON PAGE 105*

Not caring how disgusting it might be, you reach into the toilet and wrap your fingers around the object. Its glowing subsides as you remove it from the water and you discover that it's a pearl, perfectly round and beautiful.

"Ohhh!" Emma coos.

"Holy potatoes," Jake says. "It's bigger than my baseball!"

You rotate it on your fingertips, admiring the pink luster.

A noise in the hall jerks you all back to attention. The monster had been long forgotten while you'd examined your treasure. Behind you the window is only one foot wide, not large enough to squeeze through. You're trapped!

The sound draws closer. Jake begins to shake. Emma looks to you but you're all out of ideas. The shape slides into view.

"Oh hello, kids!"

"Mr. Goosen!" Emma cries. "Thank goodness!"

He chuckles. "Sorry to sneak up on you, just wanted to make sure you were okay. Have you–ohh, the *Queensland Pearl.*"

"The what?"

"I found that scuba diving in the great barrier reef in 1972, off the coast of Australia. Ran into some trouble along the way. You should have seen the octopus that tried to stop me!"

The three of you look at one another, eyes wide.

"Well, remember my rule: just one item from the house. But that's an excellent choice for a prize. Very well done! It's getting late, you had better get back to your homes."

None of you argue; your small taste of adventure was enough. You follow Mr. Goosen out of the house–thankfully without seeing any sign of the monster–and back outside.

You might have found better treasure, but you're happy to be safely away. For now, this is...

THE END

102

You point to the crates. "Those are far more exciting."

The three of you approach. The crates are *enormous*, about three feet tall and just as wide. They're made of old wooden boards nailed together. Like something out of Indiana Jones.

Jake bends down and runs a hand over the surface of the first crate. Underneath the layer of dust are printed letters in black ink:

- T - R - E - A -

"Aww, the rest is faded," Jake says. "But it looks like 'TREASURE'." He slides over to the second crate and does the same thing:

- S - T - R - I - C -

"Why didn't they use better paint?" Jake asks stubbornly.

"That just means they're *old*," you tell him. "That's a good thing. Older means more valuable!"

"Oh, yeah!" Jake realizes.

Emma moves her flashlight from one crate to the other. "So which one do we choose?"

To open the first crate, *HEAD TO PAGE 96*
To open the second crate, *TURN TO PAGE 72*

"I do *not* want to see what's in the fridge," you say, walking toward the pantry. The door creaks as you open it. You flick the lightswitch on the outside but nothing happens. Thankfully the window in the kitchen provides *some* light for you to see.

It's large enough to walk inside, so that's exactly what you do. Shelves line three walls, filled with sacks and boxes of food. Jake and Emma enter behind you.

You reach for a sack of rice when one of the boxes begins to shake. You hear the rattle of food inside, when suddenly a white mist forms behind it. The mist coalesces together and moves into the middle of the pantry...

...and forms into the shape of a floating little girl.

"HI!" she says with a strange, echoing voice. "MY NAME'S ELIZABETH!"

You stifle a scream as the ghost floats in front of you. Emma's eyes are wide, like she doesn't believe what she sees either.

"Tell me my birthday!" the ghost demands. "You'd better know it..."

To guess a random date, *GO TO PAGE 49*
If you have the pool cue, you can try to hit her *ON PAGE 104*
To run away, *FLEE TO PAGE 118*

104

You still have the pool cue from the billiards room. You grip it like a baseball bat and swing at the apparition.

It passes right through her.

"I'm a *ghost*," the little girl explains. "You can't hit a *ghost*."

Her mood changes from playful to angry. "You three are mean. I don't want to play with you. I want you to *go*."

"Okay!" Jake sputters. "We'll go! We promise!"

But the door slams closed behind you. You're in nearly total darkness now, with only a sliver of light showing underneath the door. The ghost girl begins to moan sorrowfully.

Something heavy hits you in the back of the neck. More things fall to the ground and you realize it's the bags and boxes of food, tumbling off the shelves. Jake cries out as something strikes him.

What are you going to go? *GO TO PAGE 114*

Your eyes are still adjusting to the dim light when Emma falls into the room behind you, followed by Jake. Emma closes the window speedily but softly, making as little noise as possible.

The three of you crowd your faces around the window.

After a few moments Mrs. Hollencamp appears. Her little Yorkie, named *Princess*, is almost invisible, with the leash disappearing into the tall grass. The old woman looks around the back yard as if second guessing what she'd heard. She leads the Yorkie onto the deck, too close to the house for you to see. But you can hear her footsteps on the hollow wood dwindle as she goes around the other side of the house.

"Nice thinking, Emma," Jake says. "I didn't take you for an acrobat, climbing walls!"

Emma smiles but looks embarrassed.

Jake turns his gaze to the room, eyes wide and excited. "Let's start this treasure hunt!" he says, rubbing his hands together.

Something brushes against your back, even though both of your friends are in front of you. For a second you think you hear something whisper *birthday* in your ear. You spin around, pulling your arms close to your body protectively.

Emma and Jake swivel their heads toward you. "What's wrong, Mike?"

"You guys didn't hear that?" you ask.

Emma says, "No..."

A shiver goes down your spine. Your friends are looking at you like you're crazy. "Nevermind," you say. "Let's just look around."

Explore the room *ON PAGE 47*

106

"...yeah, let's take a look at the piggy bank," you agree.

You cross the room, pointedly ignoring the cradle that continues moving at the edge of your vision. The piggy seems unremarkable, made of smooth porcelain and with a slot on the top. "Give it a shake," Jake suggests.

You oblige him. Hundreds of tiny objects, presumably coins, clink around inside.

To smash the piggy bank, *FLIP TO PAGE 134*

If you've changed your mind, try a different room *ON PAGE 117*

You climb the vines and lattice, ignoring that you're now two-and-a-half stories off the ground. Darkness has fully fallen, leaving each grasp and step dangerously blind. The wind is whipping your jeans around your ankles and your shirt around your waist. You feel around for each hand-hold, praying that it doesn't send you to your doom.

Finally your hand runs out of room to grab as you reach the attic window. It's slightly larger than a pizza, without any glass. It's completely open to the elements, but dark and foreboding inside. Distant lightning illuminates the inside for brief photographs of time.

"What do you see?" Jake calls from below. "Can you fit?"

Honestly? You're not sure. The only way to find out is to climb a little farther and give it a try.

You take another step up, reaching inside the window. Your shoulders press against the frame. You place your hands on the inside wall and give a burst of strength. Your shoulders squeeze through and you rocket into the room.

Your eyes take a few moments to adjust in the near-perfect darkness. There are large objects all around, looming over you. What could they be?

"Mike?" you hear Emma's voice drift up. "Mike? What is it?"

You don't want to be alone. "Come on up," you call down to them.

Wait for your friends *ON PAGE 132*

108

"The birthday card under the bed was to Mary," you say. "So your birthday must be May 14."

"Everyone always guesses her birthday," she says sadly. "Nobody ever remembers mine."

"I remembered," you say with a smile, although you wouldn't have known it if she hadn't give you two choices.

She smiles back up at you. "Yes! You did!" Without warning she shoots out of the fur coat and spreads her arms in a big hug. You feel a tingling, cold feeling as she passes through you. "Oh well. Maybe I'll hug you some other time. See you in another life, buddy!" she says before disappearing through the ceiling of the closet.

Whew, well at least that was over. You turn to leave when you see one of the shoe boxes on the ground glowing again, the same yellow light as before.

"Hmm."

Find out what's in the box *ON PAGE 109*

You bend down to slide the shoe box away from the wall, to get a better look before you do anything. It's beige colored and has no markings on the outside. The kind of box you'd find in your mom's closet.

Fearlessly, you pull the lid off the top.

A rectangular shape sits inside, about as long as a paperback book, but thinner. It's like a three-dimensional trapezoid, with diagonal sides instead of vertical.

And it's gold. Solid, glowing, gold. You pick it up. It's *heavy,* far heavier than you would expect of an object that size.

"Dude, what are you–" Jake says as he comes down the stairs with Emma, but he cuts off as you turn around with the gold in your hand. "DUDE."

"Ahh, the Bodyguard Bar," comes a voice from behind you.

"Mr. Goosen!" Emma exclaims.

His eyes are focused on the gold bar. He steps forward and reaches for it, but then draws back his hand. "President Eisenhower let me take a bar of gold out of Fort Knox."

"Why would he let you do that?" Jake asked.

"It was the least he could do after I saved his life!" Mr. Goosen says. "That was during my four years as a member of the Secret Service. I was much quicker back then!"

You want to ask Mr. Goosen more, but it's getting late and he ushers you all outside, though he never actually touches you. He disappears back inside and the three of you run home before it starts to rain.

Your parents don't believe where you got the bar, though the serial number on the side checks out. It's worth thousands of dollars! It's a pretty good haul, and better than you expected when you went inside the House on Hollow Hill. Unfortunately, that means it's now...

THE END

110

You sprint across the room, pulling Emma behind you. Multi-colored balls whip just above your head, forcing you to duck to avoid being struck. The ghost–what else could it be?–continues screaming as you dart through the doorway and into the hall. Jake tosses his cue on the ground as he follows.

"This way!" you say, picking a direction at random. You run to the end of the hall and stop at a door, practically throwing your body through as you turn the knob. When Jake and Emma are inside you slam it behind you.

Your ears perk up. The sound of screaming slowly diminishes, as if its disappearing into the distance. After a few moments it's completely silent.

Emma looks at you. "What was that?"

"It sounded like a little girl," Jake says. "An *angry* little girl."

"Whatever it was, it sounds like it didn't follow us," you say. You turn away from the door. "It looks like we're in the kitchen."

Explore the kitchen *ON PAGE 56*

She opens the box and starts digging through, pulling out what look like pieces of paper. You reach inside and grab a stack. "Oh, they're letters," you say, noticing the mailing addresses on the front.

"Not just any letters," Emma says. "*Old* letters. See the stamps on the corner? They say 1942."

You open one, removing the note inside. It's written on faded yellow paper, in a long, cursive hand. The writing takes up the entire page and the back side.

"They're all addressed to the same person," Jake says. "Who is Olivia Helmsworth?"

A deep, foreboding voice answers you: "My wife." The sound echoes throughout the attic.

"Who... who's there?" Emma asks.

You sense a trembling in the floor.

Uh oh. This is probably the end. *GO TO PAGE 125*

112

You wrap both hands around the bundled doll and gently begin to lift it.

Your heart stops as the crib stops rocking, and there's a sudden noise:

"Ma-ma! Ma-ma!"

The three of you jump, but then it becomes obvious that you squeezed too hard and activated the doll. At least your friends jumped too!

Holding the doll over your shoulder with both hands, you look back inside the crib. It's completely empty.

"Where is it?" you ask. "I thought for sure the baby was the right answer!"

"Dude," Jake says, pointing at the doll.

You turn it around. On the back of the doll is a paper note, pinned to the blue blanket.

"CODE: 1 - 4 - 2"

Emma cries, "It's the safe code!"

Gently placing the doll back where you found it, you rush back into the office and approach the safe. Like before, you carefully hug the wall to slide around the gaping hole in the floor, where you can see the smashed piano from earlier. "Be careful," Emma says. "Don't screw it up!"

What a note of confidence, huh?

Try the safe *ON PAGE 62*

THE HOUSE ON HOLLOW HILL

"I'm not sure what the riddle means," you say, "but my dad keeps all his valuables in his bedroom. Let's go check there."

You walk down the hall and into the Master Bedroom. A king sized four-post bed occupies the entire far wall. An antique dresser is to the left, with a mirror resting against the wall on top. There's a pile of clothes in the corner between two windows.

"So... where'd your dad keep his valuables?" Jake asks.

You go to the dresser and check in the top drawer, ignoring the puff of dust that kicks up. Completely empty. "This is usually where he hides stuff."

Jake walks over and peers inside, giving you a face.

"What about the bed?" Emma asks.

"What about it?"

"Well, you rest your head on the pillow," she says. "The riddle was: 'The path to what you THINK is most precious, is underneath what is TRULY most precious.' Your head is the most important part of your body, so underneath would be under your pillow..."

Since you don't have a better idea, look under the pillow *ON PAGE 116*

114

Desperately, you throw your shoulder against the pantry door. The wood creaks but does not budge.

You try a second time, and then a third. Your shoulder aches and you eventually give up.

"Mike, I'm scared!" Emma calls. The heavy bags and boxes continue raining down on them. Although you cannot see, you can feel the items flying in the room. It's like you're in a tornado of grocery items!

You huddle on the ground and cover your head protectively. Eventually the torrent might end, but for now you're in a whirlwind nightmare that signals...

THE END

The girl begins to weep, a soft, pitiful sound.

"Aww, there there," you say, trying to sound comforting. "I'd like to get to know you. What *is* your birthday?"

She ignores you and the wailing increases. You still can't see, but you feel the coats whipping around you violently.

"Mary, please!"

The closet feels like the inside of a tornado, zippers and fur slapping at your face. You crouch down on the ground and cover your head and ears. Soon you begin to scream, joining your voice to Mary's.

Your friends find you like that some time later.

"Dude, calm down," Jake says.

You open your eyes to the dim light of the hallway. You scramble out of the closet and look back, but everything appears normal now.

"There was... I saw... it..."

"You are *messed up*," Jake says. "Was it the ghost?"

"There's no ghost," Emma says.

"Yes! It was the ghost of a little girl!"

Jake's eyes widen. "See? I told you, Emma?"

She looks skeptical, but with Jake and you convinced you hot-tail it out of there, out the front door and down the street. Nobody will believe you at school, but Jake does, and for now that's all that matters. Well, that, and the fact that this is now...

THE END

116

You cautiously approach the bed in the dim light. Afraid you might see another ghost, you grab the pillow by the corner and whip it away.

There's nothing underneath but a pillow-shaped outline in the dust.

"Well now what?" Jake asks.

"Uhh..."

Something is happening to the bed. It begins rotating, swirling in space. It's as if someone unplugged a bathtub stopper, and the entire bed–sheets, mattress and all–is suddenly going down the drain. The center turns black, a swirling vortex of darkness consuming the room.

And you realize it's pulling you toward it.

"Get back!" you yell, but it's too late. Jake turns to run but slips, and flies backwards through the air into the center of the spinning orb. He disappears.

Emma slips and you grab her hand. She floats into the air, feet facing the black swirl while you grip her wrist tight. "Don't let go!"

"I won't," you promise, but soon it doesn't matter. The vortex pulls both of you forward, your sneakers sliding on the dust-slick wooden floor.

"Oh no!"

You eventually can't hold on any longer. With a scream Emma tumbles backwards into the vortex, blinking out of existence. You flail your arms around to stop yourself but it's no use. Soon you're pulled toward it.

Time seems to slow down as you near the center. You decelerate, as if moving through water, then jello, then sand. You don't know how long the end will take. Days, weeks. Maybe years. But one thing that *is* certain is that you have reached...

THE END

THE HOUSE ON HOLLOW HILL

"Dude, we came here for *treasure*," you decide, setting the pink porcelain pig back on the dresser. "Not a bunch of pennies."

"That's what I've been saying!" Jake agrees.

"So..." Emma glances at the moving crib. "Do you want to look inside there?"

You follow her gaze. "No, definitely not. Let's try a different room."

"But which room do you think the riddle refers to?" Emma says.

You recite the riddle to yourself: 'The path to what you THINK is most precious, is underneath what is TRULY most precious.'

Enter the Master Bedroom *ON PAGE 113*
Head back to the office by *FLIPPING TO PAGE 39*

118

You did *not* wake up this morning prepared to deal with ghosts. "Run away!" you blurt out, turning and sprinting out of the kitchen. You hear your friends close behind.

"Don't go!" the ghost calls, but you don't look back.

In the hallway you pass the door to the cellar. There's a strange gargling sound coming from within, and a greenish light glowing underneath the door. "Nope," you say, moving right past it into the Den.

Find safety in the Den *ON PAGE 71*

You can tell there's no chance to reason with her–even if she *weren't* a ghost. You turn to run.

"NO!" the girl screams.

You press your back flat against the wall so you can shimmy past the hole, but the girl jumps in front of you with a *swoosh*. She tries to grab your leg but passes right through.

"Come back!" she yells. "You have to play my *game*."

You inch along the narrow floor, eying the hole in front of you and the piano room below. It's an awfully long drop. You're not sure how you survived it before.

"PLAY WITH ME!"

The girl continues jumping through your legs, trying to stop you. And although she passes through like a hologram, you feel as strange tingling sensation in your legs.

Jake and Emma have stopped at the door to the hallway, watching. "Hurry up Mike!"

You're almost there, just a few more feet. The girl darts back and forth between your legs, and the tingling sensation intensifies. It's like when your foot falls asleep after you've sat on it too long. In fact, it feels *exactly* like that feeling...

It happens before you realize it: your foot is so numb that you can barely support your weight. As you move to take the next step your dead foot rolls forward and you buckle.

"PLAY WITH MEEEEEE..." cries the girl.

You flail around but there's nothing to grab but the flat wall. You fall forward into the hole, just like you did earlier. Except seeing as there's no cushioning on the piano, and it's smashed entirely, this time the fall signals...

THE END

120

You leave the office and walk down the hall, carefully leaping over the destroyed section. The master bedroom is the last door on the right.

As you walk inside the smell of mildew and rat droppings strikes your nose. "It smells worse in here than the rest of the house," you say. "How could Mr. Goosen have been living here?"

"It sure looks like he hasn't been here in years," Emma agrees.

A king sized four-post bed occupies the entire far wall. An antique dresser is to the left, with a mirror resting against the wall on top. There's a pile of clothes in the corner between two windows.

Two windows.

"Which window does it mean?" Jake asks.

"Does it matter?"

"I don't know..." Emma says. "After all we've been through in this place, I'm sure it *does* matter."

You pick up the small six-sided die from the dresser. "Let's let chance decide."

"Seriously?" Emma asks.

"Unless you have a better idea..."

Roll a die! If you don't have one, simply pick a number at random.

If you roll a 1, 3, or 5, *TURN TO PAGE 50*
If you roll a 2, 4, or 6, *HEAD TO PAGE 94*

"I bet it's Mary's birthday," you exclaim, remembering the card in the bedroom. "January 21." You enter each number individually, first turning the dial clockwise, then counter-clockwise, then clockwise again. Feeling pretty good about yourself, you give a confident tug on the safe handle.

It doesn't budge!

"That can't be right," you say, growing frustrated. "It has to be the girl's birthday!" You tug again and this time your hand slips on the handle.

You're tumbling backwards through the air! Except instead of hitting the floor, you're falling even farther!

FALL DOWN TO PAGE 24

122

The mist forms into the shape of a little girl, wearing a pearl-colored dress.

You look at your friends. It's time to get out of this crazy house.

"That was *wonderful*," the girl says, putting her hands on her cheeks. "Just like mom used to play!"

The comment is so random it catches you off guard. "Your mom plays the piano?"

The ghost girl nods. "Mmm hmm. She tutors kids, too."

Jake suddenly seems curious. "Say, you don't know where anything good in this house is? Something valuable?"

"JAKE!" Emma hisses.

"Of course I do!" the girl says. "In my piggy bank! It's in the nursery, upstairs." And with that she fades away, humming the piano tune.

Jake makes a face. "Piggy bank? We want treasure, not *pennies*."

You scratch your chin. "I don't know, let's go check it out. If it's pennies we can always just not take them."

Head upstairs *ON PAGE 123*

You climb the stairs to the second floor. You pass an office, a bathroom, and a little girl's bedroom before reaching the nursery. You can tell by the crib in the corner, and the arrangement of toys all over the ground. The toys look old, like from the 1960s. It doesn't look like anyone has played in there since...

"There's the piggy bank," Jake says, striding across the room. He picks it up off the dresser. It's round and pink, with a slot on the top to drop coins in. He shakes it up to his ear, and the sound of a hundred tiny objects rattles around. "Bo-ring," he says, tossing it to you.

Catching it in the air, you bring it up to your ear and do the same thing.

"Let's try the office," Jake says. "Maybe he has a computer or something..."

You continue rattling the piggy bank. There's a strangeness to the sound that's not quite right. You lift the piggy bank over your head...

Smash the piggy bank *ON PAGE 134*

124

The little girl stares at you blankly, no emotion at all on her face. Sweat beads on your forehead as you wait for her judgment. You begin to wonder if you got the answer right.

Finally she jumps up higher in the air. "CORRECT!" she cries in her high-pitched voice. "Wow! I knew you guys looked smart!"

The three of you let out a cheer.

"You've given me my freedom," the ghost says. "I can finally leave."

Leave? What, was she trapped there?

"Hey, wait a second," Jake says. "What about our prize? You said we'd get a prize if we answered all three right!"

"Of course," she says. "The prize lies behind the fires of Seuss."

"What's that supposed to mean?" Jake asks.

But it's too late. As quickly as she had appeared, the ghost girl fades away into nothing. The last thing you see is a big smile on her face.

"What a ripoff!" Jake says. "Where's our prize? We answered her questions fair and square!"

"*You* didn't answer anything," you mutter.

Suddenly the fireplace lets out a loud groan. The bricks scrape against the wood floor as the entire hearth rotates out, revealing a secret passage behind.

Emma is standing next to the bookcase, a copy of The Cat and the Hat in her hand. "It was the only Dr. Seuss book on the shelf," she says. "I picked it up and the fireplace moved."

The three of you gaze toward the dark passage.

Enter the secret passageway *ON PAGE 138*

The trembling grows in your feet, moving up your legs and buckling your knees. "We've made a huge mistake," Jake says. "I knew we shouldn't have come into the house!"

"You were the one who wanted treasure most of all!" Emma yells.

It feels like an earthquake, or a tornado outside. The trees smack against the open window from where you entered. You begin to think that Jake might have been right.

All at once it cuts off. And as you open your eyes you see a dark shape standing a few feet away.

Discover what it is *ON PAGE 126*

Trembling, Emma raises the flashlight.

It's Mr. Goosen!

"How..." you mutter. "How did you get up here?"

He laughs a deep, heartfelt laugh, as if it's the funniest joke in the world. "A better question would be how do I get out? But we'll come to that in a minute..."

"Boy am I glad to see you!" Emma says. She darts forward to wrap him in a big, relieved hug.

And she passes right through him.

It takes you a few heartbeats to realize what had happened. Emma is on the other side of Mr. Goosen, and you can still see her through his body.

"Oh," Mr. Goosen says, looking embarrassed. "I'm afraid I cannot give any hugs today, dear."

"What..." Emma says. Her face is as pale as...

"A GHOST!" Jake blurts out. "You're a ghost, just like the little girls we've seen!"

The old man chuckles at that, running a hand through his white hair. "I don't much like that term, but in effect you are correct."

"But how..." Emma stammers. "Why..."

"It's a long story," he says, glancing at the window.

Rain droplets flurry inside, dampening the ground around it. "But I suppose we have the time, now don't we? As long as you children aren't scared..."

"You're the third ghost we've seen," Jake says plainly. "We're used to it by now."

"Well okay then." He clears his throat. "It all started back when I was in the war. The Second World War, that is. I was seventeen years old then, and volunteered to join the navy. To serve my country. I'd lived on a farm before that, and it was dreadfully boring. My girlfriend was saddened to see me go, but I wanted to see the world! So I promised her when the war was over I would return safely.

"So I volunteered, but by the time our battleship arrived in France the fighting had ended. They sent us to the Pacific Ocean after that, but soon there was peace there too. I had sailed back and forth without ever leaving my ship. That wasn't the adventure I expected! So when the war ended I stayed with the Navy."

"But you promised your girlfriend..." Emma begins.

He raises a hand. "I know, I know. I felt terribly guilty about it. But I made it up to her, writing love letters every single day. I did miss her dreadfully! It can be lonely on the sea.

"But I got what I wanted. When the war was over we sailed all over the world: to the Polynesian Islands, to the Ivory Coast of Africa, to the jungles of the Indian subcontinent. I saw it all! And I collected quite a stash of treasures, purchasing a small item in every place I visited. I even sent some home to Olivia."

"Olivia..." Emma said. "Olivia Helmsworth?"

"My girlfriend back home," he nods. "And later my wife!"

"But your wife is Mrs. Goosen," Jake says.

"She wasn't always Mrs. Goosen!" he chuckles. "This was before we were married, so she still had her maiden name. Anyway, when I eventually returned home she forgave me, since I had sent her all these wonderful letters. But that was back in 1950, and she kept them all in a box after we got married. We lived in Iowa then, and later moved to Washington, D.C., then Seattle, then we settled down here to have a family. The box got moved so many times we thought we lost it."

"So... how did you become a ghost?" Jake blurts out.

"I'm getting there, I'm getting there! So we settled down here to have a family. We had two wonderful daughters, Elizabeth and Mary."

"We met them too!"

"I'm sure you did," Mr. Goosen says sadly.

"Oh," you say. "If they are ghosts..."

"Oh, it's not what you think!" Mr. Goosen says. "My girls lived happy, fulfilling lives. I may have outlived them, but they did not pass away until they were in their 70s."

"70s? But the ghosts we saw were children," you point out.

"Yes, despite their ages they always remained happy children at heart. They became ghosts from their happy, innocent childhoods! And then finally, two months ago, it came time for me. But don't feel bad! I lived to the age of 95, and had an incredibly fulfilling life. I wouldn't change a thing."

"I'm sorry," Emma says sheepishly. "We didn't even realize..."

"Don't be!" Mr. Goosen insists. "Olivia kept it quiet, knowing that I didn't want a lot of fuss. She moved out last month, to go live with our grandson Frank. And that's where you come in. I need your help."

"Ask us anything!" Emma says. "We'd love to help."

"Like I said when you entered the house," Mr. Goosen says, tapping his head, "what's up here is what truly matters. Memories! But memories fade as you age, and my dear Olivia forgot all about the box of love letters. I know it would mean the world to her if you took these to her. I've been fretting so much that my spirit has remained trapped here, trying to convince children to come find these!"

Jake frowns. "Why are your daughters trapped here, then?"

"They can tell I'm not at peace," he says. "They can feel how desperate I am to get these letters to Olivia!"

"Why didn't you just tell us what you needed in the first place?" you ask.

Mr. Goosen says, "Your motivations had to be pure. You skipped over all sorts of treasures and prizes in my house and ended up here, in the attic. You made some extremely powerful decisions tonight. You're not any group of normal children!"

You look at Jake and Emma. They both have determined looks on their faces. "Of course we will," you say. "Just tell us where she lives."

130

The next day the three of you wake up extra early before school to visit the address Mr. Goosen gave you. Even Jake skips baseball practice to help. Luckily the address is only a few blocks away!

As you approach the small, blue house, you hear the sound of piano music. "It's coming from inside," you say. "104 Pleasant Terrace. This is it."

Knock knock knock, the sound of you politely tapping on the door. The piano music cuts off, and you hear someone approach. The door opens, and a kindly old woman with gray hair and blue eyes looks down at you. "Oh hello children! I remember you from my old house, on Hollow Hill."

"Hi Mrs. Goosen," you say. You shift your feet. "This may seem really strange, but..." Not sure what else to do, you shove the box at her.

She takes it with a surprised grunt, and places it on the ground. She removes a single faded envelope and raises it to her bespectacled eyes.

She gasps.

"Where... how..." she almost looks like she's going to faint! Jake jumps forward and puts a comforting arm around her, and the three of you lead her inside. You enter a room with a piano and help her into a cushioned chair.

"Your husband wanted us to bring this box of letters to you," you explain. "He wanted us to tell you: 'I would still write Olivia every day if I could. Always remember that.'"

Mrs. Goosen reads the letter and a tear forms at the corner of her eye. "This is the most precious thing anyone has ever given me," she says. "How can I possibly repay you?"

"We already had an adventure," Jake says. "We don't need anything else. Honest."

But Mrs. Goosen shakes her head. "Wait here." She disappears in her back room, and comes back with an armful of items. "My husband left these for me to give out. He said I would know when it was time."

To Emma, she says, "This is an electric keyboard I used to practice on. You look like someone who can play!"

Emma takes the keyboard and beams.

To Jake, she hands a long wooden bat. "Be careful with this. That's a baseball bat from someone famous. Herman Babe, I think. His name is on the end."

Jake's mouth hangs open as he inspects it. "*Babe Ruth*? Oh man!"

Lastly, she smiles at you. "You must be Mike. My husband especially left this for you." She extends her fist and opens it, palm up.

Inside is a gold pocket watch. The very one Mr. Goosen had carried all his life. "Now you'll always know what time it is."

You don't know how to thank her. Instead, you run forward and embrace her. She hugs you back, warm and grateful.

As you let go, your eyes drift over to the piano in the room. "Actually, there's one more thing I would like."

Mrs. Goosen frowns. "What's that?"

"Can you give me piano lessons? The way you used to give lessons to your daughters?"

Mrs. Goosen smiles. "I'd love nothing more."

CONGRATULATIONS!
YOU HAVE REACHED THE ULTIMATE ENDING!

In recognition for taking up the gauntlet, let it be known to fellow adventurers that you are hereby granted the title of:

Hero of the Haunted Realm!

You may go here: **www.ultimateendingbooks.com/extras.php** and enter code

MH25655

for tons of extras, and to print out your Ultimate Ending Book Two certificate!

And for a special sneak peek of Ultimate Ending Book 3, *TURN TO PAGE 154*

132

Afraid to move much while you're alone, you wait for your friends to enter. Jake comes first, followed by Emma. By the time she squeezes through and falls to the floor it's pouring outside. "We might be here a while," she says, brushing herself off.

"I can't see anything..." Jake complains.

"Good thing I've got this!" Emma says, whipping out a flashlight. A cone of yellow light appears, blinding you momentarily. When your vision returns Jake lets out a big sigh.

"Boxes. More boxes. I'm *sick* of looking through crummy boxes of junk!"

You see that he's right. Occupying most of the attic, floor to ceiling, are cardboard boxes. Emma picks up the closest one–sending a swarm of small spiders scurrying from underneath–and drops it in between the three of you. "Well unless you want to go out in the rain," she says, "we might as well start looking!"

Investigate the boxes *ON PAGE 111*

You run up the stairs, taking the steps two at a time. "I wish I had paid more attention in Mr. Arrieta's class!" Emma cries as you reach the second floor.

You're in a wide open balcony area overlooking the first floor. The balcony is shaped like a square, with rooms running off of it at regular intervals. Everything is open and airy. Although the stairs were intact, the second floor balcony is not: one large section appears broken, as if a giant had smashed it through with a massive fist, leaving a five foot-wide gap.

The ghost is still making noise behind you, so you jump into the first room you see. The noise cuts off as you close the door behind you.

"I think this is an office," Emma says, looking around.

Check out the Office *ON PAGE 60*

134

You lift the pig over your head and smash it on the ground. With the sound of broken porcelain it blows up into a thousand tiny pieces.

The sound shocks Jake. "What'd you do that for?" he demands. "It's just dumb coins."

Emma's eyes widen. "No. Jake, look!"

Among the pink porcelain pieces are tiny, colorful objects. They look like skittles, until you lean forward and pick one up. It's blue, with at least a dozen smooth, flat surfaces. "It's a sapphire," you mutter.

"They're gemstones!" Emma cries.

The three of you pick up the sapphires and rubies, emeralds and topaz, exclaiming as you find larger and larger gems. You fill your pockets with them until they're overflowing and you have to carry the rest in your cupped hands.

"*Now* we can get out of this house!" Jake says. None of you disagree.

As you exit out the front door you see Mr. Goosen standing there, waiting. "Ahh, the gems from my days in the mines of Svalbard!" he says when he sees what's in your hands. "What a prize. Just about the best thing you would have found..."

You thank him and hurry down the street; it's already getting dark. The gems are surely worth thousands of dollars. You can't wait to show your parents. Maybe now they'll let you and your brother go to space camp.

It was an exciting adventure, and the three of you never tell anyone about the strange things you saw in the House on Hollow Hill. Nobody would believe you, anyways. Excited about what the future brings, you accept that this is an exciting way to reach...

THE END

"I know this one," you say. "It's one of the most famous book lines in history. Moby Dick."

The little girl squeals with joy and does a spin in the air. "That's right! I knew you'd be good at this game."

Jake gives you a congratulatory pat on the back.

"QUESTION TWO!" the ghost says, holding up the peace sign. "What was Mark Twain's real name?"

Jake stares. "That *is* his real name."

"No," Emma says, "it was just a pen-name. Ugh, I just learned this! It's on the tip of my tongue..."

They both look at you.

If your answer is Samuel Beckett, *TURN TO PAGE 141*
If your answer is Samuel Clemens, *FLIP TO 66*

136

You recognize it immediately. "It's the code we found in her diary!"

"Hey, that's right!"

Careful to avoid the hole in the floor, you return to your friends and spread the scroll out on the floor so you can all read. "Just move each letter forward three places," Emma says. Each of you begins decoding it in your head, and soon the message is clear:

TO FIND THE ULTIMATE PRIZE, CLIMB OUT THE MASTER BEDROOM WINDOW

"Climb *out* the window?" Jake says.

"That's what it says..."

"Well?" you ask. "What are we waiting for?"

What *are* you waiting for? *TURN TO PAGE 120*

The little girl's face, so hopeful and smiling, immediately drains away. "You were so close," she whispers, eyes pale and wide. "I thought you would get it right. I thought you would *free* me."

Thinking fast, you say, "I'm sorry. I got confused. Give us another chance. Please?"

But the little girl is shaking her head. "No. There are no second chances. We'll have to wait for the next group of kids to come inside."

Next group of kids? What does that mean?

Before you can ask, books begin flying off the shelves, spreading open and fluttering in the air. They crash all around you like a barrage, a constant torrent of paper and leather.

One book hits you in the head. You fall over and hold your temple, feeling dizzy.

Emma stands over you. She's shouting something, but you can't quite make out the words. Your ears feel filled with cotton. The room spins around you. *Maybe I should read more,* you think, wishing that this wasn't...

THE END

The passageway is actually a stone staircase leading underground, away from the house. It's dark, but a torch on the wall abruptly flares to life with fire.

The three of you look at one another. That's the *least* crazy thing that's happened to you tonight.

You lead the way down the stairs, holding the torch ahead of you. Shadows slide back and forth as the flame flickers. The air grows cold and damp.

The staircase ends, opening into a small room. There's a stone pedestal in the center of the floor, standing about waist-high. There's something large resting on top.

You approach cautiously. The object is square, and shining in a strange way. You hold the torch over it but can't see much.

Emma gasps. "That's a Gutenberg Bible!"

You can see she's right:

"What's that?" Jake asks.

"It's one of the most priceless items in the world," Emma says. "Less than 50 exist!"

Rather than take it out yourselves–you're afraid to touch it–you send Jake back to get his parents. Then it's a rush of authorities: first police, then museum curators and historians. The discovery makes national news, and you're all on TV. You even receive an enormous prize, which you split among you. Even Jake was happy, then.

All in all, it was quite the adventure. Sometimes you wonder what else you might have found in that house, but you can't think of anything more valuable than the Gutenberg Bible. "Maybe we'll find another haunted house to explore," you tell Emma one day. She laughs. "One is plenty."

You laugh, nodding. After everything you've been through, you're happy to say this is...

THE END

There's a low, hollow sound–like wind blowing through cracks in a window. You think it's getting louder. Is that the ghost? It's tough to be certain.

Jake whispers, "*What was–*" but he cuts off as you put a finger to your lips.

The howling wind sound grows louder. The only light comes from underneath the door, and even that is dim. You stare at it, waiting to see if the light changes at all. Which seems silly, since a ghost probably wouldn't dim the light at all if it passed in front. But the idea of ghosts seemed silly before you got here, so you stare anyways.

The sound seems to be inside the room, just on the other side of the door. You feel your heartbeat pounding, louder than anything else in the closet. You close your eyes and wait for the door to swing open, or the ghost to appear.

Then the howling sound begins to diminish. Slowly, like the volume is being turned down, the sound fades away.

Jake swallows. "What was that?"

"I think we all know what it was," Emma says. For once even she seems shaken.

"It was a little girl. Named Elizabeth." You tell them about the encounter down in the closet.

"We should get out of this house," Emma decides. "This is too much."

"But what about our prizes? I don't want to leave here empty-handed," Jake says, although his protest sounds weak.

They're both looking at you for a decision.

"Let's all calm down," you say. "The ghost is gone. And she didn't seem *that* scary. It was just a little girl." It feels weird pretending like seeing a ghost was no big deal.

"Then what's the plan?" Emma asks.

Stick around and explore the closet *ON PAGE 53*
Or, head back to the Master Bedroom *ON PAGE 146*

140

The piano shakes menacingly, causing the wires inside to make a cacophony of noise. The chaotic music fills the air, until a strange mist begins rising off the back of the piano.

You know what's going to happen by now. The mist forms into the figure of a little girl, wearing a faded white dress. And you can see straight through her into the ceiling beyond.

The girl is extremely unhappy. "No! It's wrong. All wrong!" She bobs up and down in the air. "Mom played it *much* better than that. *She* never made mistakes!"

She starts crying, a long, sorrowful wail. The sound causes a sharp pain deep within your ears. You cover your head with your hands but it doesn't help.

You fall to your knees in agony as the girl's cries intensify. You send one final look at Emma as darkness begins closing in all around you. "I'm sorry!" you try to tell her, right as you realize this is...

THE END

"Ohh!" you say before Emma can speak. "It's–"

"No, wait!"

"–Samuel Beckett," you finish with an emphatic stomp.

Emma sighs. "No, that's not it at all!"

"But Samuel Beckett sounds familiar."

"He was a *different* writer."

Jake tugs on your arm. "We've got problems here."

The ghost girl is bobbing up and down angrily, waving her arms. Wind picks up in the room even though the windows and door are closed.

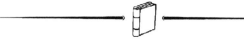

Endure the girl's fury *ON PAGE 76*

142

Feeling strange for trusting a note you found under a doll that must have been made before World War Two, you enter the code. Clockwise to 1, counter-clockwise to 4, then clockwise back to 2. You take a deep breath before turning the handle.

It opens with a soft *click*.

Your friends cheer behind you, but you're too focused on the safe. As light enters, the object inside radiates color on your clothes and the floor. It's like a thousand rainbows shining. After the darkness of the house it's brilliantly bright. Your eyes adjust and the object comes into focus.

It's a small tiara of yellow gold, some parts spun so thin and intricately that it appears fragile. Multi-colored gems cover the face, ending at a green emerald at the pinnacle. Now *this* is some treasure!

"What is it?" your friends call.

You step out of the way so they can see. Emma gasps. Jake's mouth hangs open. Everyone is awestruck.

"What's that next to it?"

You turn back and see a small roll of parchment on the floor of the safe. It's six inches long and bound with a wax seal. "I guess it's a note, or scroll, or something."

"Bring them both over here!" Jake says impatiently.

You nearly grab the objects, but then remember Mr. Goosen's warning: *only take one thing*.

Which one do you grab?

If the tiara is your kind of treasure, *GRAB PAGE 35*
Or, indulge your curiosity by opening the scroll *ON PAGE 144*

You take a look at the rack of suits, which have both coat jackets and pants on the same hanger. Some of them are business suits, blue and grey and tan, with matching neckties. Others are tuxedos, black with shiny lapels and bow ties, and perfect creases down the pant legs.

Not sure what else to do, you begin patting down each suit. The first one has something soft inside the coat pocket, which ends up being a wadded up tissue. You toss it aside and wipe your hands on your shirt–better be more careful.

The next suit has some fancy cufflinks on arm. You make a mental note to come back to those. One jacket pocket is filled with quarters, while another has a faded valet ticket.

You're patting down the fourth or fifth suit when you feel something more solid inside a jacket pocket. It feels heavy, and is definitely not a used tissue.

Feeling cautious, you call your friends over. Jake pokes the outside of the jacket and squints in concentration. "I think it's shaped like a square."

"What is it?" Emma asks.

"Are you sure we should reach inside?" you say. "What if it's... I don't know. What if it's dangerous?"

"Why would it be dangerous?"

It's a good question, but after all the other craziness of the house you still hesitate.

Reach inside the pocket *ON PAGE 152*
Or, leave the closet *ON PAGE 146*

144

Although the tiara is a wonderful prize, your curiosity nags at you. You've come this far, so you might as well go for broke!

You grab the scroll and turn back to your friends.

"Dude, what are you *doing*?" Jake asks.

"I've got a hunch," you say. With a dramatic gesture, you grip both ends of the scroll and open it in front of you.

The entire message is gibberish.

"What the..." you mutter. "I can't read any of this. It's nonsense."

"Read it out loud!" Emma says.

"No really, it's gibberish!" you insist. "The first line is:

'RQH WKLUWB-VLA'

Jake scrunches his face. "That makes no sense."

If you know the code, *TURN TO THAT PAGE*

If you cannot decode it, *TRY PAGE 34*

You've seen enough scary movies to know playing a game with a ghost is *never* a good idea. "Hey, is that Casper?" you say, pointing at the bottom of the closet.

The ghost tilts her head down.

You bolt from the closet. The ghost cries out, "Hey! WAIT!" but you don't slow down, rounding the corner and running up the steps two-at-a-time. Your shoes slide on the dusty wood, and you nearly fall, but the ghost's pursuit keeps you moving fast.

You reach the top just as Jake and Emma appear from the office. "Mike! What are you–" Emma begins, but she cuts off as you grab her arm and pull her down the hallway.

Jake must see the ghost, because suddenly he lets out a yelp and follows.

The ghost's voice follows you along: "Come back! I only wanted to *play.*"

You lead your friends to a random door. Thankfully, it's not locked. The fancy wooden dresser and the four-post bed means it's obviously the Master Bedroom. There are some windows on the far wall, and two doors on the right. The far one has a tiled floor–it's probably the bathroom.

You open the nearest door. "In here! *Quick!*" Your friends dart inside, and you're right behind them, swinging the door closed behind you.

Everyone is silent, except for the sound of panting. You cock your ears to listen for the ghost.

Hold your breath *ON PAGE 139*

Cautiously, you open the door to the closet, cringing as the hinges creak. You look around the bedroom. Everything is still.

You go to the door to the hallway and close it. That wouldn't stop a ghost, but it makes you feel safer nonetheless.

"I don't want to leave just yet," you say, "in case *it* is still out there. Let's look around."

The dresser is antique, and covered in a thick film of dust. You open the top drawer. It's empty, except for a dead spider curled up in a ball. The next drawer is the same.

Jake's standing over the bed, holding one of the pillows in his hand.

"Bathroom's empty," Emma says, wiping dust from her hand. "There's an old electric hair dryer, but that's it. Jake? Are you okay?"

Slowly, Jake shakes his head. "I picked up the pillow, and I thought I saw something moving. The *bed* moved, like we were on a boat. But then it stopped."

Emma smacks him on the back. "I think all this dust is getting to your head."

"I saw it!"

"Hey guys," you interrupt, looking out the window. The glass is cloudy, but you can barely make out some shapes. "There's a balcony out there."

They join you at the window. Jake presses his face against the glass and says, "Weird. There's no door to access it."

"We could open one of the windows," Emma smiles. "Let some of this *dust* out."

Jake makes a face and grabs the base of the window. It scrapes the side of the pane, and barely budges, but then finally relents and opens wide enough for you to crawl through.

Crawl onto the balcony *ON PAGE 150*

Books are your specialty. "We'll play your game," you blurt out.

"But Mike!"

"I've got this," you assure her. "Trust me."

"OKAY!" the ghost girl squeals with excitement. "I'll ask you three questions. If you get all three right, you'll get a prize!"

"Three?" Jake sputters. "I don't know..."

"QUESTION ONE!" the girl announces, holding up one finger in the air. "What famous book begins with the line, 'Call me Ishmael'?"

If you think it's Moby Dick, *TURN TO PAGE 135*

If you think it's Pride and Prejudice, *GO TO PAGE 86*

148

You examine the rack of dresses. Most of them are wrapped in protective plastic, like they just came back from the dry cleaner. You feel weird looking at people's clothes, but hey, Mr. Goosen said he'd already taken everything he wanted out of the house.

The first dress is a faded pink color, with long sleeves and a wide waist. The hem is woven with intricate lace. It looks like something someone would wear in the 1920s.

The next dress is much newer. It's bright blue with thousands of sparkling sequins all over the front, with padding built into the shoulders.

The third one is covered up inside an opaque bag, and is much larger than the others. You pull the zipper down the side of the bag and take a look inside. The dress is a light gold color, almost silver. Ribbons are tied in bows in two columns down the front, with curtain-like lace strewn between them. More bows are woven up around the bodice and neckline, and the sleeves are loose and just long enough to cover the shoulders.

"Woah," Emma says, gently pulling the dress out of the bag. She finds a tag near the hanger. "Look at this symbol!"

V. R

"What does V.R. mean?" Jake asks.

The door flies open, and you all jump back with fright until you see that it's Mr. Goosen. He has a big smile on his face. "V.R. means Victoria Regina."

Jake has a confused look on his face. "Regina?"

"Regina is the Latin word for queen," Emma says. Then her eyes widen. "That means this dress belonged to..."

"That's right: Queen Victoria of England! That was a gift to my wife a very long time ago. It was her favorite dress. Ahh, the balls we used to go to." Mr. Goosen gets a sad look on his face, but then it disappears. "You've made a wise choice for your prize."

"What? I don't want a dress!" Jake complains.

"Dude, Queen Victoria died a century ago," you say. "That dress is probably priceless!"

"Quite so!" Mr. Goosen says. "In fact, that's one of the most valuable items in this house!"

Emma carefully puts the dress back inside the protective cover. Mr. Goosen leads you downstairs and outside, explaining that the best thing to do would be to contact several prominent museums–the Smithsonian, the National Gallery in London, and several others you've never heard of–and hold an auction so they can bid on the dress. "Something that old, and in such good condition, will fetch a pretty penny!" he explains. Even Jake seems awed by the thought.

It might be a while before you can hold such an auction, since museum curators from around the world will need to be gathered, but you decide it's a fantastic ending. You take one final look back at The House on Hollow Hill and smile that you've reached...

THE END

150

Night is falling, so it's now difficult to see. You lean one foot out the window until you feel the balcony with your toes. Then you duck through, stepping down with your other foot. Thunder rumbles in the distance.

Now you're on the balcony with a row of six potted plants in front of you.

Your friends crawl through after you. The balcony rocks on old wood, but holds your weight. "There's nothing out here," Jake complains.

"Hey," Emma points. "That pot is different."

"Different how?"

"The soil in the other pots is grey and dry. Old. *This* soil is new. See how black and moist it is?"

"So what?" Jake says.

"Don't you think that's weird?"

"I think this entire house is weird."

"Maybe there's something inside," you suggest.

"Why would someone hide something inside a flower pot?" Jake asks.

"Hey, you said it yourself. This entire house is weird."

"Then stick your hand inside, Mike."

You step up to the pot. The brown ceramic is chipped with age, as if the flower pot has been there for decades. But the soil is definitely new. You reach toward it...

Before your fingers touch the soil, a small green bulb appears, the size of a thumbtack. It pushes aside the soil and rises an inch out of the pot. "Woah," you say.

"That's some strong fertilizer!" Emma says.

But the plant doesn't stop there. It continues rising until it's a long vine. It's unable to support its own weight, so it flops over the edge of the pot and continues growing. It extends toward your foot, and begins to wrap around your ankle. With a yelp you shake it off.

More vines begin appearing from the soil, three, eight, ten. Soon dozens of them are crawling out of the pot and moving across the balcony. You step back from the writhing vines, too shocked to say anything.

Your back hits the balcony railing. You've run out of room, and the vines are still moving. One of them crawls up the wall and into the bedroom, blocking off your retreat.

"What do we do?" Jake asks.

You look behind you. It's a ten foot drop to the ground.

"I have an idea," you say.

Emma licks her lips nervously. "Tell us!"

"You're not going to like it."

The three of you turn to face the railing, and the ground below. Emma gives you a 'you've got to be kidding' stare.

"Do you have a better idea?"

The vines are spreading impossibly fast, brushing up against your shoes. There's no time. You lift your left leg over the railing, touching down on the balcony lip on the other side. Then you do the same with your right leg, so that you're on the other side of the railing. You hold on tight. Suddenly the drop seems *much* farther than before. Doubt begins spreading in your mind.

A vine pushes through the railing, wrapping around your calf. Moving with instinct instead of thought, you jump.

It feels like you fall forever in the darkness, until your feet slam into solid ground with a loud *THUNK*. You fall forward on your hands, but overall seem to be okay.

You're on a wooden deck that spans the length of the back side of the house. You get to your feet and call, "Come on, guys!"

The vines add urgency to their evacuation, and they both drop down a moment later. You help them up. "That was close!"

"It still is!" Jake says. You look up and see the vines pouring over the side of the balcony in your direction. How could a plant grow so *fast*?

"This way!" Emma yells, running into the back yard.

You follow her through the tall, unmowed grass toward the woods. Thunder booms across the sky, and the tall pines sway back and forth wildly. Fat raindrops begin to fall.

The woods provide a sense of safety after the dangers of the house. You enter just as the rain begins falling in earnest. The three of you stop at the third tree you come to, breathing heavily.

"What was that?" Jake asks. "Plants don't do that!"

A shadow appears from behind the tree. Its voice is deep and jarring. "Maybe not the plants *you've* seen..."

Prepare to defend yourself *ON PAGE 12*

152

You don't know why you're so cautious, but you shake it off. You take a deep breath, pull apart the suit jacket, and reach inside the breast pocket.

You feel a cold texture, and grab the object between two fingers as if it's radioactive before pulling it out.

"A wallet!" Jake says.

It's a faded piece of leather folded in half, thick with what must be paper bills. On the outside of the leather is printed a coat of arms:

"Check to see if there's any money!"

You turn it sideways and open it, then carefully pull apart the sides of the bill holder...

It's paper alright, but not paper money. They appear to be notes, grocery lists written in ink, receipts from various restaurants. You pull them out and toss them on the floor until the wallet is empty. "Aww, man!" Jake says.

The door flies open, and you all jump back with fright until you see that it's Mr. Goosen. He has a big smile on his face. "Even if that wallet was filled with hundred dollar bills, it would hardly increase its value!"

Emma cocks her head. "What do you mean?"

"I wouldn't mind a few hundred dollar bills in there..." Jake says.

Mr. Goosen says, "You see, that wallet once belonged to a very important person. A man with the title of Prince of Wales."

"Where's Wales?" Jake says. "Is that even a country?"

"Wales is part of the United Kingdom," Emma says. "The Prince of Wales is Prince Charles, the son of Queen Elizabeth! He's the next in line for the throne!"

You stare down at the leather in your hand. Suddenly it seems far heavier than before.

"Very good!" Mr. Goosen says. "I served in the Royal Navy with Charles four decades ago. He had no need of a wallet, seeing as he has servants and assistants following him around everywhere. You don't need to carry money or a photo ID when you're one of the most famous people in England!"

Jake's mouth hangs open as he examines the wallet. "But don't *you* want the wallet?"

Mr. Goosen purses his lips. "Where I'm going, I won't have need of a wallet either. Don't worry. It's much better off with you three."

He leads you out of the house–where you see no more ghosts, thankfully–and outside. The wind is blowing the trees all around, but there's no rain now. It's strangely calm.

A wallet from Prince Charles! You're not sure whether to keep it, auction it off, or donate it to a museum. But regardless of the future, you're pleased with the prize, and smile to have reached...

THE END

154

SNEAK PEEK

Welcome to Outer Space!

The year is 2260, and the solar system has long been colonized by the Earth World Coalition and the Mars-Jupiter Alliance. Space thrives with ships of all shapes and sizes – building, exploring, and discovering.

You are Lt. Colonel ANDON MERCER, space marine. Together with first mate and co-pilot SERENA VALENTINE, the two of you fly the Kestrel, a Codec-class scout ship tasked with patrolling the outer edges of known space. Every day is the same: quiet, routine. Every day up until now.

"Lieutenant Colonel," a voice calls from inside your helmet. "This is Commodore Garriott of the EWC Blackthorne."

It takes you less than a second to open a channel. "I read you Commodore. Go ahead."

"A ship has appeared on the outer edge of the belt," he tells you. "Unknown origin. All attempts to hail it have failed, and our scans are coming up empty." The Commodore pauses. "Right now, you're closest."

A new waypoint blinks to life on your screen. He's right. It's not far at all.

"Orders?"

"Your orders are to intercept, board and investigate," the Commodore continues. "At least until we get there."

"Roger that," you reply. Your terminal rapidly begins filling with information as Serena plots your newly-adjusted course. "Anything else, sir?"

"Yes, Lieutenant Colonel. Use caution."

"Affirmative."

In no time at all you're accelerating past cruise velocity, speeding through space on a direct intercept for the derelict ship. Over the rim of your faceshield you shoot Serena a sideways glance.

"Ready for this?" you ask.

"Are you kidding?" she smirks back. "Been waiting forever."

At full thrust it doesn't take long to reach the edge of the asteroid belt. You squint through the blackness of the Kestrel's viewport and watch as the strange, derelict ship floats into view.

"One of ours?" you ask.

"Hard to say," Serena replies. "It's certainly not a design I've ever seen. And it's transmitting on a totally unknown transponder code."

Except for a few distant running lights the ship appears dark and silent. Your console tells you two things: it's moving at a very high rate of speed, and it's heading directly for Earth.

"Hail it."

"I've been hailing it for ten minutes," Serena tells you. "No response."

You look down again at your console, which reads green across the board. Although much larger than the Kestrel, the strange vessel seems bent on ignoring you. For right now at least, it poses no discernible threat.

"Coming around."

It takes some maneuvering, but you manage to slingshot alongside the sleek, dark ship. As you get closer you can see that it's definitely Earth-made. There's a name stenciled across the bow:

DAUNTLESS

Serena brings you out of your trance with a tap on the shoulder. She points one finger to an external airlock.

"Any other ideas?" you ask.

"Not offhand."

"Fine then. Let's go."

"Docking procedure initiated," you tell your co-pilot. "Grab onto something."

From here the computer takes over, calculating the complex set of maneuvers needed to exactly match the derelict ship's speed and direction. You feel the Kestrel shudder through a final series of thrust and counter-thrust micro-adjustments, and then the docking clamps engage with a hollow boom.

Squinting at her hand terminal, Serena's brow furrows. "That's weird..."

"What is?"

"I'm getting no atmospheric reading in certain parts of the ship," she says. "Either they sustained damage, or they dumped most the air."

Serena is cut off by the sharp hiss of hydraulics. The airlock cycles through an array of yellow and green lights, and then the door slides open with a shift of internal pressure. You give your own ship one last reassuring pat and push on through.

The world beyond the airlock is cold and dark. As your eyes adjust, the outline of a room fades into view. Condensation in the form of ice crystals clings to control surfaces and shadowy computer consoles. Everything is in standby mode; all panels are dark except for the red-orange glow of emergency LED's.

The ship is dark, spooky, and deserted.

"I can make my way down to Engineering," Serena suggests. "If I can get the power up we can restart the air scrubbers. Get some atmosphere going in here."

"Probably not a good idea until we know what we're facing," you say, drawing one of your service pistols. "Might be better to stick together until we've secured the ship."

Serena holds up a black box with red and yellow wires protruding from it. "Or I can hook this battery up to the mainframe computer in the Ops room. Make the ship tell us what happened here."

Which way will *you* proceed when you explore...

THE SHIP
AT THE
EDGE OF TIME

ABOUT THE AUTHORS

David Kristoph lives in Virginia with his wonderful wife and two not-quite German Shepherds. He's a fantastic reader, great videogamer, good chess player, average cyclist, and mediocre runner. He's also a member of the Planetary Society, patron of StarTalk Radio, amateur astronomer and general space enthusiast. He writes mostly Science Fiction and Fantasy. www.DavidKristoph.com

Danny McAleese started writing fantasy fiction during the golden age of Dungeons & Dragons, way back in the heady, adventure-filled days of the 1980's. His short stories, The Exit, and Momentum, made him the Grand Prize winner of Blizzard Entertainment's 2011 Global Fiction Writing contest.

He currently lives in NY, along with his wife, four children, three dogs, and a whole lot of chaos. www.dannymcaleese.com

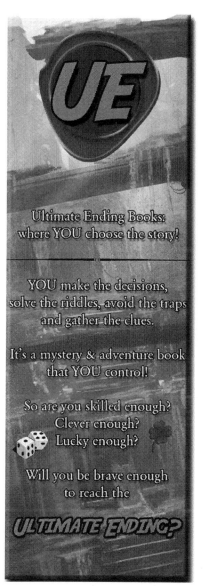

Made in the USA
Middletown, DE
22 November 2018